the BOOK of CHAOS

STARFELL BOOK ONE

JESSICA RENWICK

Published by Starfell Press

Starfell Book One:
The Book of Chaos

Copyright 2018 @ Jessica Renwick. All rights reserved.
Contact the author at www.jessicarenwickauthor.com

ISBN (hardcover) 978-1-7753871-3-8
ISBN (paperback) 978-1-7753871-0-7
ISBN (eBook) 978-1-7753871-1-4

Cover Page design by Ebook Launch
Edited by Talena Winters
Formatted by Red Umbrella Graphic Designs
Proofread by Erin Dyrland.
Author Photo © Bonny-Lynn Marchment. Used by permission.

Printed in the United States of America, or the country of purchase.

The Starfell series:

The Book of Chaos

The Guitar of Mayhem

The Bow of Anarchy

The Curse of the Warlock (2021)

The Star of Truth (2022)

Other works by Jessica Renwick:

The Haunting of Lavender Raine

The Witch's Staff (part of the Mythical Girls anthology by Celticfrog Publishing)

Praise for The Book of Chaos

"Author Jessica Renwick has crafted a highly engaging tale about the love of family and the true bonds of friendship. This enchanting tale offers a thrilling adventure for young readers who are sure to be entertained by this first book in the Starfell Series."
– Children's Literary Classics Book Awards & Reviews

"Renwick has designed an imaginative world for her story with rich details without letting description getting in the way of action. Book One of this series is a quick, delightful read that leaves you wondering what those kids will get up to next!"
– Karina Sinclair, editor at Line by Line Studios.

"Renwick weaves a wonderful story filled with twists and turns and exciting new characters that are definitely going to draw in even the most reluctant readers in your household."
– Patrick McNulty, author of the Milo Jenkins: Monster Hunter series.

2019 Children's Literary Classics Gold Award Winner for Middle Grade General

2019 Book Excellence Award Winner for Children's Fiction

2019 Story Monsters Approved

For every person facing the scary monsters in their own lives.

"Believe in yourself and all that you are. Know that there is something inside of you that is greater than any obstacle." – Christian D. Larson

Please note: I have put together a glossary of unfamiliar words, names, and world-specific terms. This is located at the back of the book.

Prologue

Endora huddled over the sleeping toddler's crib, the deep hood of her cloak blocking the moonlight from her face. The once-vibrant pinks and florals of the girl's room were muted by late-night shadows. While a soft breeze came in through the open window, it was not the cause of the chill in the air.

She gazed at the child, who was sleeping in blissful ignorance of the danger lurking above her. Endora caressed the child's plump cheeks, ripe and sweet as summer peaches, then touched her own hollow, sunken ones. She glanced at her hands, waxy skin hanging off her bones like rags. She had been beautiful once, long ago. And she could be beautiful again. She just needed nourishment. She drew in the alluring smell of youthful energy. Beauty and new life were there before her. The temptation was overpowering.

The old woman ran a sharp, ice-cold finger over the girl's fine hair. *I could take her with me now and be done with this . . .*

"M-mistress." A small toad-like man with bulbous eyes in an oversized tweed jacket tugged at her robes. The stench of rotting cabbage permeated the filthy jacket, giving him watery eyes and a runny nose. "I hear its guardian coming," he said. "Methinks you ought to stash the Collector now. We must hurry!"

The old hag snarled and raised a skeletal arm at the creature, gloating as he squeaked in fear and cowered below her. The sound of soft footsteps came from the floor downstairs. She lowered her arm.

"Very well, Arame."

Tamping down her hunger, she gazed at the child. She should wait. The girl was still too young. She wasn't ready yet. As much as the haggard woman hungered for youth and sustenance, such a small soul wouldn't fulfill that need—and what a waste it would be.

Endora turned away from the crib. Ten years from now, when the child had grown fully into her bloodline, the Blood Star would fall. Then, the child would be ready. Then, Endora's patience would pay off.

Glancing into the mirror on the wall, she shuddered at the sight of her sickly face. She prodded at her sagging cheek with a bony finger. Soon she would be lovely again, as fair as her younger years, but with the wisdom and power that only comes with age.

She rubbed her hands together at the thought. "I simply need to find other peaches to pluck while I wait for this young fruit to ripen."

Arame shrank into his oversized jacket. She ignored him and snapped her fingers in the direction of the door. The lock clicked into place.

She reached inside her cloak and pulled out a large leather-bound book—her masterpiece. She ran her fingers lovingly over the sprawling vines painted on the cover. If her enchantments had worked, to the casual eye, they would look like regular garden vines, crawling up and enveloping the cover of the book.

Only upon close inspection would one would see that these vines were covered with sharp thorns and blackened, rotting leaves. Trapped inside their growth, various bones and human skulls writhed. The skeletons appeared to be struggling to break free, but the tangled roots offered no hope of escape. The book pulsed with the heat and energy of a conscious, hungry beast. It sensed something important was about to happen.

The footsteps reached the bottom of the stairs and with them, a lullaby. It was sung by a motherly voice, full of love and contentment. As the footsteps started up the stairs, the old woman glanced around the room and smiled when she saw the bookcase in the corner. She had to place the Collector perfectly, where it would blend in, the enchantment veiling its true appearance until the time was right.

The door handle rattled. The child awoke and looked around. When she spotted the strangers in her room, she began to cry.

Arame hopped from one foot to the other, making odd croaking sounds and waving his webbed hands at the rattling doorknob. The singing stopped.

"What on earth?" The child's aunt pounded on the door. "Is somebody in there? Fable!"

Endora stepped to the tall bookshelf against the wall. The Collector would fit in perfectly among the magical bedtime tales of princes, goblins and faraway kingdoms. The untrained eye would slide right over it, searching for more exciting stories to fall into. She placed the book on the highest shelf, wedged between *A Tale of Two Trolls* and *The Sleeping Squonk*. The book sighed, nestling itself in for a long nap.

Perfect. She grinned in wicked satisfaction.

The child's aunt sounded near hysterics. "What's going on in there? Fable?"

Endora whirled towards her companion.

"Arame, now!"

He stepped forward and Endora grabbed his head and pulled him towards her, wrapping him in her cloak. Looking up at his mistress, he croaked twice, blinked three times, and licked his bulging left eye. With a poof of foul-smelling green smoke, they were gone.

The leather-bound book sat smugly in its place on the highest shelf. The door burst open and a tearful lady in a fuzzy, pink bathrobe rushed into the room. She picked up the wailing child and snuggled her tightly to her chest. Consumed with comforting her niece, she didn't seem to notice the hint of green mist slowly evaporating from the room. The book watched as she rocked the child in her arms, vines curling around its spine in a nasty smile.

ONE

Rose Cottage

F able Nuthatch watched the candle in front of her extinguish with the wave of her hand. From her seat on the hardwood floor of the bedroom she shared with her younger cousin, Timothy, she twisted her other hand near the flame and it flickered back to life. She watched in mystified delight as the dancing light cast long distorted shadows on the floral wallpaper, transforming their normally-cozy room into a ghostly cavern. Painted by the grasping shadows, the hand-sewn quilts, comfortable armchair, and large oak bookshelf in the corner looked like they belonged in a haunted house, not the pleasant bedroom of Rose Cottage.

"You know what my mom would say if she walked in." Timothy frowned, his hazel eyes taking on their characteristic you're-going-to-get-me-in-trouble glare. "She doesn't like you playing with magic. Or candles." He glanced nervously at the door from his perch on his tidy bed.

1

Fable ignored him and continued to toy with the flame, blowing an annoying tress of her smooth chin-length black bob out of her eyes with a dismissive grunt. Timothy was almost four years younger than her, that age where a younger sibling—or cousin—becomes an irritating shadow. He was always hiding rocks in her shoes or stealing her favourite books, and he was constantly begging her to play with him.

"Come on. It's late. Mom will be here any minute." Timothy crawled under his covers. His mousy brown hair fell over his eyes as he stared at her in the dark. "Turn on the light. Let's pick a story."

Fable sighed and snuffed out the candle with a flick of her wrist. She didn't understand how she did these odd things like bending light, moving the air around her, and encouraging plants to sprout between her fingers. It came naturally for her. She only had to concentrate on the candle for a moment, and the flame was hers to control. Not that she would tell anyone other than Timothy about it—Aunt Moira would never allow it. "Having magic" was only one entry on Fable's list of oddities, right after her dark purple eyes—but much more problematic.

She stood and turned on the light switch next to the door. Aunt Moira would be up the stairs at any moment to tuck them into their beds. Even though Fable was twelve-and-a-half years old, her aunt still hovered and fretted over her like a hen over her newly hatched chicks.

Fable had lived here with Aunt Moira and Timothy ever since she was a toddler—right after the accident that had killed both of her parents and Timothy's dad. Moira always said that the reason she moved them to this country cottage in the middle of nowhere had nothing to do with her previous life of adventure and magic. But Fable didn't believe her. Why else would they be in Larkmoor, the only place in all of Starfell where nothing exciting ever happened, and where magic was certainly not welcome?

Grimm, the children's constant companion, let out a loud *whoof!* from his bed between the door and Fable's nightstand. The enormous mastiff licked his chops with a dopey grin, drool hanging down to the cushion.

"You're such a good boy." Fable stroked his soft fur and gave him a kiss on top of his head.

Moira had gotten him to protect her and Timothy, but Fable sometimes wondered how effective he would be if something actually threatened them. Despite his impressive size, he seemed much more likely to roll over for a belly scratch then to growl menacingly at an intruder.

3

Despite his questionable ability as a guard dog, Grimm was an excellent test subject for Fable's spells. Over the last few years, he had modelled many different colourful shades of coat, green being Fable's favourite. She was quite sure it was his, as well. She would never forget the look on Aunt Moira's face the day an emerald mastiff greeted her at the door. Or the hundreds of slugs Fable had picked off the garden cabbages as punishment.

His tail thumped against the floor as he grinned up at her, tongue lolling out to one side. Fable had once read that every good dog needs at least three hugs per day. She figured that Grimm, being the best dog around, should get at least ten. Both children made sure he got them.

The door opened and Aunt Moira entered the room with a tray holding three cups of tea, her bangles tinkling lightly as she moved. It was their nightly routine. Moira liked to say that there was nothing better than a cup of mint tea and a story to help settle a person down for sleep.

After she laid the tray on the nightstand next to Timothy's bed, Aunt Moira scanned the bookshelves for that night's tale.

"What will it be tonight?" She asked, her long skirt swishing as she climbed the step stool to see the top shelves. "Tales of pirates, or princesses, or great quests through the Windswept Mountains?"

Wisps of dark hair that had escaped her bun stuck out around her head and looked like a strange crown in the shadow it cast on the books. She always reminded Fable of a fortune teller. All she needed was a crystal ball and she'd be ready to tell Fable her future.

"Pirates!" Timothy said with a wide grin on his face.

Fable groaned. She'd heard those stories dozens of times. She focused on the top shelf. A large black book with golden script slid slowly out of the spot between *The Bogwater Princess* and *Sunflower Acres.*

"Fable, that's enough," Moira said.

Fable smiled endearingly at her aunt. "'Tales of The Black Forest' hasn't been read in ages. It's feeling left out."

"Hmm . . ." Aunt Moira pursed her lips. The corner of her mouth twitched. She turned back to the books in front of her and ran her hand along the titles, her bangles making a comforting jangling sound.

The shelves of the bookcase were filled with every kind of adventure a child could dream of. Books that brimmed with magical, distant lands. Stories of love, war, and exotic creatures. The books were disheveled, with no method of organization, and yet somehow,

Fable always managed to find just the right one. She'd spent hours sitting on that ragged green rug in front of the bookcase, immersing herself into other lands and magical journeys.

Just when Aunt Moira had chosen a title and reached up to grab it, a book from the top shelf toppled out from its spot. With a rustle of papers, it hit Moira's head and fell to the floor.

"Fable!" Aunt Moira straightened her glasses and rubbed her head.

"I didn't move that one," Fable exclaimed. "I swear!"

Moira shook her head and bent down to pick up the large vine-painted book.

"Strange, it doesn't have a title." She opened the book and flipped through the pages. "Or words. The pages are blank."

Fable perked up, peering at the book her aunt held. Her imagination raced. "Maybe it's a spell book." She ignored Timothy's snort.

"The last thing you need is a spell book." Aunt Moira snapped it closed. "Odd we haven't seen it before."

"Maybe a book fairy hid it for me."

"Us." Timothy glared at Fable.

Aunt Moira raised her eyebrows, a small smile on

her lips. "There are no such things as book fairies. We must have skipped over it before, up there on the top shelf. It's just a sketch book, meant for drawing. If you want it, I'll leave it down here for you."

She placed the book on top of the dresser.

"Now, back to finding a story." Aunt Moira stepped back onto the footstool, muttering titles to herself under her breath as she searched.

Fable picked the leather book up off the dresser. She held it in her lap and gazed at it with wonder. Dark vines crawled over the cover, glistening in the lamplight. Fable touched them and they felt warm on her fingertips. A faint hum radiated from its pages when she opened the cover.

"Aunt Moira . . ." Fable leaned in to listen. Yep. She definitely heard it.

"What about the one with Princess Daisy?" Moira asked.

"No!" Timothy sat up on his knees. "No more stories about princesses."

Fable closed the book. The humming stopped, but the cover shuddered. It rose and fell under her fingers.

"Aunt Moira, I think this book is breathing."

Her aunt shook her head and didn't turn away from the bookshelf.

"That's impossible, Fable. Books aren't alive."

"But—"

"Here we go! This one's about a knight." Aunt Moira plucked a dark red book with a shiny dragon on the cover from the shelf.

Timothy cheered. Moira sat down in the pink armchair between the bookcase and his bed and began to read.

Fable stared down at the book in her hands. It lay still, acting just like a book should. Her mind must be playing tricks on her. She put the book back onto the dresser and picked up her tea from the nightstand. She was soon lost inside the castle from her aunt's tale.

Trouble on the Trail

F able sat under the large maple tree in the backyard of Rose Cottage. The tree's long branches, with pointy leaves that reminded her of stars, hid the sun's hot summer rays. She sat with her legs straight out in front of her, knees barely covered by the hem of her dark purple dress. The strange leather book lay open in her lap. She peered into its empty pages—her hair falling into her face for the umpteenth time—and chewed on a pencil, then dropped it into the pencil box on the ground beside her. She tucked her hair behind her ear, wishing she had pulled both sides back with barrettes instead of just one.

It was the summer holiday, so the children were on their own during the day while Aunt Moira worked at the nursing home in Larkmoor. Her shifts were long, but she reminded them every day that she was never far from reach in case of an emergency—which hadn't happened yet in the nine years they'd lived at Rose Cottage.

Fable and Timothy spent their days playing or reading in the backyard. Or, in Fable's case, practicing magic. This happened under the watchful eye of Grimm, with his ever-loving, albeit drooly, presence.

Fable had been trying to write in the book all morning. No matter what kind of writing tool she used, the words faded away to nothing before she started the next line. She had tried blue ink, black ink, pencil, and even felt marker. She picked up a green crayon from her pencil box and wrote *Magical books for magical girls* onto the empty page. The green letters vanished, absorbing into the paper.

Timothy appeared next to her wearing plastic sandals, neon-green swim trunks and a sleeveless white t-shirt. His face was flushed from the heat and sweat glistened on his forehead.

"This heat is killing me," he said. "Want to go down to the creek?"

Fable ignored him, picked up a pencil crayon, and continued to draw in the book. The petals of her daisies faded from the pages.

"Fable." Timothy grabbed the pink pencil from her hand.

"Hey!" Fable glared at him, reaching for the pencil.

He laughed and held it out of her range.

She growled, putting her hands on her hips. "Give

it back."

"Come on. I'm so bored." Timothy tossed the pencil into the box and squatted beside her. "If you take me down to the creek, I'll give you my ice cream after supper."

"Tomorrow's too," Fable replied.

"Deal."

Fable closed her pencil box. Aunt Moira would be livid if she knew that they had left the yard. She was firm that they stay within the fenced boundary of Rose Cottage at all times. But as long as they made it home before five o'clock when she walked through the front door, she would be none the wiser.

Fable smiled to herself, thinking of a lazy afternoon laying in the shade of the forest, dipping her toes in the cool creek water. She closed the book and slid it into her book bag. She loved that bag—heavy dark blue wool covered with silver star patches sewn in perfectly disorganized order. She never left home without it.

"Fine." She got to her feet and slid the bag's strap around her shoulder. "But if you splash me this time, you're going in. All the way over your head." She shoved his shoulder playfully.

"Yeah, we'll see about that." Timothy ducked away from her and trotted towards the gate.

Fable whistled at Grimm, who lay napping in the

shade near where she'd been sitting. His tail wagged in response, and he heaved himself to his feet.

The children crunched through the dry summer grass to the white gate at the back of the yard, Grimm strolling along behind them. Flowering vines, wilting in the summer heat, sprawled over the white picket fence. Timothy swung the gate open, and they started down the path leading to the creek.

He chattered as they walked, telling Fable about the new video game he hoped Aunt Moira would get him for his upcoming birthday. Fable wasn't surprised. Whenever he wasn't busy blasting apart aliens or driving race cars, his hand-held video game console was either in his hand or his back pocket.

Fable's mind drifted. She only half-listened to Timothy talk about the new game as she wondered about the mysterious book and what to do with it. Despite Aunt Moira's disbelief, she knew the book had some sort of magic. Pencil and ink didn't just fade away into nothing. It had to go somewhere.

Fable's attention was dragged back to the present by a boy's loud, grating voice.

"Look what we have here."

Two teenage boys emerged onto the trail ahead, walking toward them. Fable recognized the boys, from a few grades ahead of her in school, as Duncan and

Peter. They were big for their age, with cruel smiles and hard eyes.

Fable survived school by keeping her head down and pretending not to hear her classmates whisper as she passed. And she definitely avoided Duncan and Peter, the worst bullies in the school. They would often shove kids into lockers, steal lunches and toys, and there had been one incident involving poor Adam Warbler and the school toilet.

Duncan, with his flaming red hair that blazed like fire in the sunlight, cracked his knuckles and stood wide to block the path. "Look, it's the Weird Brothers."

Duncan's sidekick, Peter, snorted at the joke, his greasy brown hair poking away from his head in clumps. The stench of unwashed boy reached Fable, and she wrinkled her nose. He looked like he hadn't showered in a week.

"Oh, good one." She pretended to laugh out loud. "My feelings are so hurt that you think I'm a boy. What gave it away? The purple dress?" She snorted. "And we are not siblings. Dimwits."

She tried to push past them, but she was small for her age, much smaller than these boys, and Peter easily pushed her backwards off the trail.

"Well, you look like a boy with your bushy eyebrows," Duncan said. "And you are definitely weird."

"Not as ugly as this one, though." Peter stalked over to Timothy and used both hands to send him toppling to the ground.

"Hey!" Timothy scrambled to stand up, but Peter laughed and pushed him back down.

Fable clenched her fists. "Leave him alone!"

Peter sneered at her. "Or what?"

Grimm growled and charged forward, the hair along his back bristling. He rushed to Timothy and stood over him, teeth bared at his charge's attacker.

Peter backed up a few steps and glanced at his friend.

"Or our dog will get you," Fable said, glaring. She stepped back onto the trail, hands on her hips. Anger boiled in the pit of her stomach.

"If your dog even touches us, my dad will be at your place tonight to deal with him." Duncan's face twisted in a snarl. He caught sight of her book bag. "What you got in there? Bedtime stories?"

"Bedtime stories for little babies," Peter added with a laugh.

Duncan reached out to grab the bag off of Fable's shoulder, and a raging heat flared inside of her.

Duncan pulled on the bag's strap.

Peter gaped. "What's wrong with yer eyes? They're

all glowy."

Her control fractured. She fixed Duncan with a piercing gaze, anger bubbling up her throat in a molten torrent.

"Get away from me!"

As she screamed, a powerful wave of energy blasted out from her. Duncan's feet flew into the air and he landed in the thorny bushes behind him with an "oompth!"

A luminous aura of greens, purples, and blues shimmered out from the spot where her magic hit the boy. It waved over Grimm, who wagged his tail and chomped at the colourful ripples.

"What the heck was that?" Peter backed away from them, his eyes wide. "You're going to hear from my mother about this!"

He turned and ran without looking back. His friend still struggled in the thorn patch and was left behind.

Fable spun around to face her cousin. The motion made the bag slip from her shoulder, so she used her hand to steady it.

"Ouch!" She snapped her hand away.

The book inside was hot. She opened her bag and peered inside. The book nestled in the bottom, a faint red glow radiating off the leather. The vines painted on the cover moved, thrashing along the spine. Fable scrunched up her face, mesmerized.

Timothy's shout broke her trance.

"That was awesome!"

Fable looked up at her cousin. Timothy had regained his feet and was pumping his fist into the air.

She stared towards the exultant boy in confusion. Behind Timothy stood an enormous bear, rearing up on its hind legs. A big brown bear with a dopey grin on its face and a . . . wagging tail?

A yell rang through the air. Fable spun around and saw Duncan—now untangled from the bush and with eyes as wide as saucers—turn on his heel and run down the trail away from them. She'd never seen him move so fast.

The bear let out a confused "whoof" that caught her attention. It was Grimm. His hindquarters slowly rose into the air as his form shifted into the familiar mastiff.

Fable's jaw dropped. She forgot all about the book.

THREE

If Dogs Had Wings

Timothy, unaware of the floating dog behind him, jumped up and down in excitement. "How did you do that? You've never been able to—"

"Timothy . . ." Fable stared at the hovering canine.

Grimm seemed to realize he was off the ground and pawed at the air. He looked like a floating, wrinkly carnival balloon, panting happily as he floated even higher. He was now even with Timothy's head.

"What?" Timothy blinked at her.

"Grimm!" Fable pointed behind him.

Timothy turned around and stood face to face with the dog, who rolled onto his back in the air. Grimm's ears and jowls drooped towards the ground, and drool hung from them in long, slimy ropes. With a big upside-down grin, he licked Timothy from his hairline to his chin. Startled, Timothy wiped the saliva from his face with his arm.

"Grimm!" He grabbed at Grimm's collar. He missed, and the dog floated higher into the air, drifting off towards the trees.

The children ran after him. Both of them jumped and grabbed at his collar and his paws. He floated above their heads. His tail swung wildly in the air as he rolled in circles.

"Grimm . . . come back . . . now!" Fable panted so hard she could barely speak.

"Come back, boy!" Timothy said.

Grimm floated off the trail into the thick of the forest and bumped into a spruce tree. Luckily, a branch caught his collar and held him in place upside-down. He stretched lazily, his paws straight up in the air. Fable and Timothy stood under the tree and stared at him in dismay. A plop of drool landed in Fable's hair.

"Now what?" Timothy asked.

Fable wiped the drool from her hair and thought. The tree was large, with long thick branches sprouting from its twisted trunk. She walked around the base of the tree and squinted up through the foliage. A stout branch grew right below the hovering dog.

Fable started to climb.

"What if you fall?" Timothy yelled.

"Do you have a better plan?" Fable shouted back to him. She grabbed onto the branch above her and heaved herself up. Higher and higher she climbed, ignoring her cousin's cries for caution.

She reached the branch she had been aiming for and came face-to-face with her dog. Grimm snuffled a happy greeting. He stretched his forelegs over his head and lapped at the air with his tongue, trying to lick her.

Fable grinned at the happy-go-lucky dog. "Grimm, you silly beast."

She stepped out onto the thick branch, holding another one above her for balance. After being sure it would hold her weight, she shimmied along towards him.

Grimm licked his nose and whined. He struggled to turn his head to watch her progress, but a twig held his collar in place.

"Hang on buddy, don't move." Fable reached out towards him. Stretching her arm as far as she could, she could just touch his paws with her fingertips. She dropped her arm in frustration.

Grimm gazed back at her with liquid brown eyes that seemed to say, "It's okay, Fable. I know you're trying."

A squirrel chattered above them. Fable glanced up, and the little creature threw a pine cone. It bounced off her forehead.

"Ouch!" She glared up at the squirrel.

It chattered back at her angrily.

"What's happening?" Timothy yelled from below.

"Are you okay?"

"I'm fine," she called back, rubbing her head.

Grimm growled. He strained to see the chattering squirrel. Spying it out of the corner of his eye, he gave a loud bark and tried to lunge at it. All he succeeded in doing was wriggling in the air. The branch holding his collar creaked from the stress.

Grimm's struggle had shifted him closer to Fable. She grabbed for him and missed, losing her balance. Flailing, she caught hold of the branch above her. A furry brown club hit her in the face.

"Grimm!" She swatted at his tail. He thumped it back and forth over her face again. She took hold of the hairy weapon in her hand.

It dawned on her that she had a hold of him. The wrong end, and his collar was still tangled in the branch, but she had him. She wedged herself against the tree for balance, gripped his tail with both hands and called out to him.

"Grimm! Get that squirrel! Get him!"

The squirrel squealed and sent another pine cone spinning through the air. It bounced off Grimm's nose. He barked and shook his head, his collar still snagged in the tree.

"Come on, buddy, you can do it!" Fable urged him on. She clung tightly to his tail.

From his spot on the ground, Timothy caught onto her plan and joined in.

"Come on, Grimm! Get him!"

That was enough for Grimm. He twisted his neck and heaved against the branch with his body. The twig snapped, freeing his collar. His restraints gone, he tried to lunge through the air towards the squirrel, but his body only floated slowly. The squirrel disappeared into the branches above. Grimm snorted.

Fable's mind raced. There was no way she could climb down the tree without letting go of Grimm's tail, and then he would float off again. But if she jumped, they would float gently down to the ground. Wouldn't they? She chewed her bottom lip. Finally, swallowing her fear, she jumped.

They hovered for a moment. Fable frowned, worried that her weight wasn't enough. She hung from the dog's tail with visions of them floating up and away towards the clouds like Penelope the Mouse holding onto the string of a helium balloon—one of her favourite stories.

And then they began to sink. Slowly, the earth crept closer to her feet.

Timothy watched with a big grin on his face. Fable sighed, grateful that nobody else was around to see her hanging from the tail of a giant, floating mastiff.

They approached the ground, but before they landed, their descent slowed and stopped. Fable stretched out her toes, but the earth stubbornly stood at least two feet below them. Her weight wasn't enough to pull Grimm all the way down.

Timothy reached above his head and grasped her hand. He pulled her to the ground and took hold of Grimm's tail. Between the two of them, their weight was enough to hold him down.

"What're we going to do with him?" Timothy asked, glancing anxiously at the dog.

"I think it'll wear off after a bit." Fable hoped she was right.

"Mom isn't going to be happy."

Fable didn't respond. The cabbages were free from slugs at the moment, but she knew some other tedious chore likely awaited her. What would it be this time? Hand-watering all of her aunt's flowers? Or worse, washing out the compost bins behind the shed?

The two guided the bobbing Grimm back to the main trail. Peter and Duncan were nowhere in sight. Fable tried not to think about what the boys would tell their parents about the confrontation they'd had earlier. She was sure that her explosive reaction to Duncan would get back to Aunt Moira, and she had no idea how to explain it.

"We'll deal with that when it comes." She said to her cousin with a weak smile. "Let's get home and get Grimm inside so he can't float off anywhere. And hope the magic wears off quick."

Grimm grinned down at them from between his front paws.

A trickle of heat warmed Fable's side where her bag rested. She tried to ignore it. She would worry about the book later.

They walked down the trail back to Rose Cottage, each child with a hand stretched high above their heads, gripping the tail of the large furry beast who lazily hovered above them.

The Enchanted Garden

"I'm so sorry, Mrs. Snipe, it won't happen again," Aunt Moira said into the phone. "I can assure you, your son won't see her again this summer."

Fable stifled a groan. She sat at the kitchen table, watching her aunt pace back and forth across the room. Moira shot pointed glances in Fable's direction as she spoke. It was evening, and Moira had just arrived home from work. Her phone had rung before she even put down her bag.

Fable heard Mrs. Snipe's loud, high-pitched voice shriek through the phone about a monster of a child who had attacked her darling son, Duncan, "out of nowhere" on the trail that afternoon.

Fable knew it was bad. As Aunt Moira tried to calm the woman, her face blushed into a soft shade of apple and then deepened to the shade of a beet fresh from the dirt. Fable and Timothy had not only left the yard without Moira's permission, but Fable had used magic in public. Even worse, she'd used magic on another

24

person. And on top of that, Grimm had suffered the consequences.

"Thank you for letting me know, Mrs. Snipe," Aunt Moira said. While her voice sounded calm, Fable knew better. She envisioned steam rising off her aunt's head. "Again, I am so sorry. I have no idea what got into her."

Aunt Moira pocketed her phone. She turned to Fable, who stared at the table, bracing herself for the lecture.

"Do you have any idea how much trouble you are in, young lady?" She waved her arms as she spoke, which made her bangles rattle. Her hoop earrings swung like a headsman's ax as she shook her head.

Aunt Moira stomped over to the sink. She jerked open the faucet, filled the kettle with water, and slammed it onto the stove. "Sneaking out of the yard, blasting other children off the trail, blowing up poor Grimm."

Grimm, from his seat beside the door, hiccupped. He rose a few inches off the floor. Aunt Moira stepped over and pushed him back down onto his bed.

"I got him back—"

"It doesn't matter." Moira pointed at her niece. "You can't use magic here. You shouldn't be playing with it at all! It's dangerous, as you proved today. And if those children had seen Grimm . . . do you realize what could have happened?"

She yanked a green owl-shaped ceramic mug off the shelf above the counter. Its furrowed brow and wide eyes glared right at Fable.

Fable gulped. Then, as though the light had shifted, she saw her aunt's worry—the tension around Moira's eyes, the frizzy hair falling loose from her bun, the jewelry jingling on shaking arms. Aunt Moira shook the owl in Fable's direction, glaring, and the moment was gone.

Like the breaking of a dam, her aunt's expression melted and her eyes softened. She placed the owl mug down on the counter.

Fable's throat thickened.

"I almost had to go to their homes and adjust their memories," she said, her voice quiet. She dropped a mint tea bag into the cup. "Do you know how serious that is? Thank goodness I was able to convince Duncan's mother that you just pushed him into the bush. But had there been more witnesses . . ." Her voice went up an entire octave. "I don't even want to think about it!"

She walked over to the table, sat down across from Fable and locked eyes with her. Fable glanced away and fidgeted with her hands in her lap.

"This is serious. You cannot practice your magic."

Fable's gaze shot back up to her aunt's face. "You don't understand—"

"I understand more than you think," Moira said. "It's not safe. It's especially not safe in front of outsiders. They aren't like us, they don't have magic, and they fear it. If your . . . *talents"*—she cringed at the word—"are discovered, we'll have to move. Do you want to do that to us?"

"I'm sorry! I didn't mean for it to go off." Fable gritted her teeth. Tears threatened to escape her eyes. "Duncan pushed Timothy down. If Grimm hadn't stepped in—"

"I know what those boys are like. It's still no excuse. You can't use magic on them. Or anybody. You shouldn't have been out on that trail to begin with. It's not safe."

"You can't be serious! I'm twelve years old, I'm not a baby. You can't hover over me forever." Fable pushed her chair back and stood up from the table. She caught sight of her reflection in the window above the sink. Her cropped hair stuck out in every direction. Her face was the same shade of beet as her aunt's.

She couldn't give up her magic. It was a part of who she was, it flowed through her veins and every aspect of her being. If she tried to suppress it, the magic would act out violently. Just as chaotic, or even more

27

so, than today. Why didn't Aunt Moira understand?

"My magic is who I am. You've never liked me. I'm not even yours."

Aunt Moira flinched and tears sprang to her eyes. She pursed her lips and crossed her arms. Her expression hardened.

"You and Timothy are never to leave this yard. You know that. Every day for the rest of the summer, I will have a list of chores for you to have done by the time I get home from work. There will be no TV, no video games, and certainly no magic. Understand?"

Fable nodded, her chest tight. Her aunt was serious, the discussion was over. After a long silence, the kettle started to whistle, and Moira got up from the table. With her back turned towards Fable, she filled her mug.

"Please go upstairs to your room and send Timothy down to see me."

Fable got up from the table and walked towards the stairs. She paused beside Grimm. He looked at her with his droopy eyes and let out a small whine. Fable scratched his ears to let him know it wasn't his fault and continued up the stairs. Grimm rose and padded softly after her.

When she got to the room she shared with Timothy, she flopped down onto her stomach on the bed. The dog leapt up and rested his head beside her. Timothy

28

looked up from his video game console, a digital tune filling the air.

"It's your turn," she said into her pillow.

Timothy slipped from the room and descended the stairs.

Fable reached down and pulled her book bag off the floor and onto her bed. She took out the empty book with the vines that writhed over the cover. It hummed as she ran her fingers over the paintings.

"I won't stop my magic. I can't," she said. She wasn't sure if she spoke to herself, Aunt Moira, Grimm, or the book. "I can't."

Fable opened her eyes to the sound of footsteps and a soft voice outside her window. She looked over at Timothy. He snored in his bed, and Grimm slept soundly beside him. They were sprawled out on top of the blankets in the heat of the night.

Fable's feet landed on the hard, wood-planked floor. She crept to the window and peered out into the night to see who, or what, was outside.

The full moon lit up the scene below her. She could clearly see the warped, aging garden shed, the weathered fence, and the overgrown garden. The maple tree's star-shaped leaves fluttered in the wind.

A petite figure in a dark cloak walked slowly around the edge of the garden. A sweet, otherworldly-voice reached Fable's ears. A woman. Fable's mind ran wild.

Maybe she's a witch.

As the woman paced along the fence, she chanted in a language Fable had never heard before. Soft wisps of blue light flowed from her hands, leaving a faint trail behind her as she walked.

Fable strained to hear the words. It was a beautiful, mournful song. Her eyelids drooped as she listened to the entrancing hymn.

Feeling dizzy, she shook her head to clear the fog in her mind and reached out to steady herself. Her hand knocked into an unlit candle. It fell from the windowsill and hit the floor with a thud. Fable's mind jumped back to reality. *What's going on? Is the song a spell to keep us asleep?* She peeked back out the window.

The woman in the yard stopped chanting. She glanced up at Fable, and a jolt of recognition passed through her.

It was Aunt Moira.

Fable backed away from the window. *What is Aunt Moira doing out there?* Fable tiptoed back to her bed and crawled under the covers.

Her aunt had spoken of magic in the past, but Fable had never seen her perform it. She felt queasy, afraid to look again. Would Aunt Moira bring this up in the morning?

She reached for her book, but her fumbling hands pushed it down between her mattress and the wall. Too tired to search for it, she decided to fish it out in the morning. Outside, the chanting began again.

Her eyes closed and her mind stumbled into her dreams.

Dreams and Reality

Fable ran in a blind panic through the forest, coughing on the acrid smoke that hung in the air. It was night, but the sky glowed an eery shade of orange. Heat roasted her back as she ran.

It wasn't the fire she was running from.

Her heart raced. Dark energy writhed through the trees. Chasing her. Teasing her like a cat with a mouse. Getting closer.

Her toe caught on a root and she fell. She hit the ground and moaned, air wheezing from her lungs. She curled her knees to her chest. Smoky black tendrils wrapped around her body. Fable clawed at the smoke entangling her, trying to free herself.

A cloaked figure emerged from the smoke and looked down at her. The face belonged to someone long dead. Waxy skin and sagging flesh hung from the skull. Decayed, broken teeth grinned garishly from sunken, bony cheeks.

The deathly face bent over her. Fable froze, her

heart in her throat.

"Fable Nuthatch," the being said with a hiss. It lowered its face until Fable could see the flames dancing inside the purple irises—eyes just like hers.

Fable woke up screaming. She opened her eyes, but the smoky tentacles from her dream still surrounded her.

She shot upright and her chest expanded, a strange feeling of both comfort and pain. A bright white light burst out from her, surrounding her and the bed. The tendrils curled and twisted, shrinking away from her. She could hear them shrieking in her head as they rolled down under her bed.

They were gone. The light faded out, leaving Fable gasping in a mess of tangled blankets. Her wrist throbbed, red and swollen from the tendrils that had touched her.

Sweat poured down her face, and her whole body shook. She was afraid to move. Strangely, nobody else in the house seemed to be awake despite her cries. Not even Timothy or Grimm—they still slept peacefully on Timothy's bed. She switched on the bedside lamp on her night table. The light twitched and flickered, creating warped shadows on the wall behind it.

She cautiously peered over the side of her bed at the floor. There was no sign of smoke or wayward tendrils. Gingerly, she hung her blanket over the edge. It hung limply, touching the floor. Nothing sprawled out from beneath her bed to grab it.

Her nightmares had started a year ago. This one was the worst she'd ever had. In all of them, she ran from a fire. However, this one was different from the rest, she'd never seen any creatures before.

Fable couldn't shake the feeling of unease when she remembered those eyes. The same colour as the ones in her mirror every day. The same amethyst eyes that made her stand out among the other children in Larkmoor.

She had certainly never awakened to something trying to strangle her before. She shook her head and swung her feet over the bed, her mind filled with fog. *Was it just a dream?* Still dazed, she wasn't sure what was true. Nothing was out of place in the room.

Her feet touched the cold floor. *Whatever's after me came from under this bed.*

Fable laughed at herself. That was ridiculous. Her mind was playing tricks on her, like a small child afraid of the dark. Maybe she'd burned her wrist on the stove earlier that day? She couldn't remember. A quick peek under the bed would ease her runaway imagination.

She grabbed her bedside lamp and held it in front of her face as she peered under the bed. She was greeted by dust and cobwebs, and the odd sock that she'd given up as gone for good. She was about to pull the lamp away when she saw a glimmer near the far wall, almost out of her reach. She swung the lamp forward and caught a reflection off a dark, square shape.

"What on earth?"

She put the lamp down and crawled halfway under the bed. Reaching with both arms, she managed to grab the object. With a wiggle and a heave, she scrambled backwards and sat up on her knees.

It was the book.

Fable traced the design on its cover with her fingers, following vines along the spine. In all the arguing and drama of that day, she'd forgotten how it had burned earlier. How the vines came alive after her magic went off. She bent her head to look closer. The vines flowed and danced across the cover. Green shoots and tendrils lashed out towards her.

The vines morphed into rotting leaves and she pulled her fingers away as though burned. Her fascination turned to disgust as a human skeleton appeared in them, struggling to break free. A feeling of horror crept over her, but she couldn't tear her gaze away from the book and the terrible scene.

The book grew hot and began to vibrate. Soft grey smoke wisped out from the pages. Heat seared across

35

Fable's hands, and the trance broke.

She screamed, throwing the book across the room. It hit the wall beside her bed with a thud. She gasped. White light shot from her hands and hit the book with a loud crack. It whimpered, the edges of its pages curling up under the cover.

Grimm lunged off of the bed and onto the floor, his hair bristled and his teeth bared. He snarled.

"It's okay," Fable said to soothe the dog. Grimm turned to her and snuffled her mussed-up hair. He placed himself between her and the book.

"Fable?"

She turned to her cousin.

Timothy's eyes were wide with fear. He sat upright in his bed, clutching his blanket to his chin. His hair stuck up in all directions, and there were pillow lines on his face.

"That book's not normal."

"I'll say."

Fable got to her feet. Her hands shook as she rummaged through the top drawer of the dresser. Her fingers found the soft leather belt she was looking for.

You can do this, she told herself. She held her breath as she carefully picked up the book. It was cold to her touch now, the scorched pages the only sign of the earlier chaos. She wound the belt around it, cinched it tightly, and buckled it closed. Then she walked over to the closet and threw it in. It fell far in the back. Trembling, she closed the door.

Fable crawled into Timothy's bed. His wide, unblinking eyes stared at her from a ghostly-white face. Wrapping her arms around his shoulders, she hugged him.

"It's okay. We're okay."

"That thing just attacked you!"

"We'll deal with it tomorrow," Fable said. "For now, go back to sleep."

She lay down next to him and he snuggled into her shoulder. She tucked the blanket up over them. Grimm leapt up onto the bed and sprawled out at their feet.

"Good boy, Grimm," Fable said.

He snuffled her hand and soon started snoring.

Try as she might, her mind couldn't go back to sleep. Her eyes never left the closet door until sunrise.

The Book of Chaos

When Fable sat down for breakfast the next morning, Aunt Moira was puttering around the kitchen, whistling a cheerful tune as she placed steaming plates of pancakes in front of the children. All seemed to be forgiven, and there was no mention of Moira's late-night song. Fable wasn't about to bring it up, not when her aunt was in such a good mood. Even Grimm, despite being underfoot and causing Aunt Moira to side-step and fumble, was rewarded for his drooly grin with a big fluffy pancake.

Fable's mouth stretched wide in a yawn. Her chin rested on her arm on the table. Timothy's head bobbed as he fought to stay awake. They both had bags under their eyes, and Fable's unruly hair was even more disobedient than usual. She tried to flatten the cowlick above her left ear, but it popped back up in defiance. She hoped the cheery yellow of her dress would make her look more awake than she felt.

"You two look exhausted." Aunt Moira sat down

with her own stack of pancakes and poured sticky, sweet maple syrup over them. "Were you up all night partying without me?"

Fable rolled her eyes. "I had a silly dream. Nothing serious." She picked mindlessly at her breakfast. Her stomach ached, and the thought of food made it worse.

"A dream? What about?"

"Nothing. It's not a big deal."

Timothy jerked his head sideways at her over the table. There was no way she was going to tell her aunt what really happened. She knew Aunt Moira would blame her magic. It would just make things worse than they already were. She would deal with the book herself.

Timothy swallowed a bite of syrupy pancake. "Actually, something odd—"

Fable kicked him under the table. He closed his mouth, his face twisted into a scowl.

"It was just Grimm being stupid," she said.

Aunt Moira looked at Timothy for a second, then shrugged her shoulders and they finished their meal with nothing more said about it.

"Make sure you don't leave the yard today." Aunt Moira stood up from the table and put her dishes in the dishwasher. She pointed to a piece of paper on the counter with a column of text in her familiar, neat

39

handwriting. "I left a list here for you. I'd like these tasks completed by the time I get home."

Tasks. Fable let out a loud sigh. Tasks were Aunt Moira's code for *chores*. As if it would be more fun to do a *task* over a *chore*.

"If you two do a good job, maybe tonight we can order pizza." Aunt Moira grabbed her purse, which was hanging beside the kitchen entrance. "I'll see you tonight." With a quick smile, she rushed out the door.

Timothy got up from his seat and walked to the counter. He picked up the list. "Weed the turnips, prune the vines, clean the algae from the fish pond . . . ugh!"

He hated working in the garden. He'd hated it ever since he was a toddler, when Fable had tried to use magic to pull the carrots and one had shot up his nose. Fable smiled as she remembered how Aunt Moira couldn't fathom why he would stick a carrot up his nose. She'd had to use pliers to get it out.

Fable scraped her breakfast into Grimm's dish. He sniffed at it and dug into the syrupy mess, his tail wagging. She scratched his ears in welcome.

When she looked up, she was face to face with Timothy. His arms were crossed.

"What are we doing about the book?"

"Don't worry about it. I'll deal with it myself."

Fable pushed by him and placed her dishes in the

dishwasher. He didn't have the spark of magic that his mother and Fable had. He'd tried but had never been able to so much as flicker a candle. Much less destroy a murderous book.

Timothy followed her. "You can't do this alone." His freckled nose wrinkled in concern. "I was there when it went off. I know what it can do."

Fable spun around to face him. "You don't have magic. You can't help. It's my book and I'll do it myself."

"Who said it's yours?" Timothy bolted for the stairs outside the kitchen entry. "Last I checked, it didn't have your name on it!"

He ran up the stairs.

"You little brat," Fable muttered under her breath and bounded after him into their room.

Timothy stood in front of the closet, his hand on the knob. He swallowed, staring at the door.

"Oh, let me do it." Fable marched over, pushed his hand from the door and wrenched it open.

The book lay innocently on the pile of laundry on the floor. It looked just like a regular book, no tentacles or menacing smoke. Fable shrugged and picked it up. It was cold and still. Very book-ish and not scary at all.

She held it up in front of her and noticed that the pages were still blackened and curled at the edges.

Proof that last night's horror was not just a dream. She kept the belt buckled snugly around it, closed the closet door, and picked up her bag.

"What're we doing with it?" Timothy asked.

Fable wracked her brain for ideas. She'd read many stories about magical items, but never anything about disposing of an evil book.

"Well, since it gives off smoke, maybe we can get rid of it with water?"

Timothy's eyes lit up. "The well!" he said, referring to an old well in the woods behind Rose Cottage. "Nobody would ever look down there. Even if the water doesn't destroy it, it's so deep, that book of chaos would never get out."

Book of Chaos, the perfect title for such a monstrous tome. Fable grinned. "That's the best idea you've had in a long time. Probably ever."

"Let's go." Timothy glanced at the book in her hands. "That thing gives me the creeps."

The children raced down the stairs to the back door. Bright sunlight blinded Fable when she opened it. It was going to be another hot, sunny day. She, Timothy and the ever-attentive Grimm made their way to the back gate along the garden walkway. They passed the rows of turnips they would weed later—after they got rid of the book.

"Let's be quick. We can't let anybody see us," Timothy said when they reached the gate. "Mom will kill us if she finds out we left the yard."

Fable glanced at Timothy in exasperation. "I know." She pushed on the gate and took a step forward. Her knee hit solid wood.

"What the—"

She rattled the gate, but it wouldn't budge. A glimmer of blue swirled in the sunlight. She reached her hand over the gate to open the latch from the outside. Or rather, she tried. Her hand hadn't travelled more than a few inches over the top of the wood slats before she hit her knuckles on what felt like a wall. An invisible, but very solid, wall.

Fable walked along the fence, dragging her hand along the invisible wall. "She trapped us in. Of course! That's what she was up to last night."

She stood in the middle of the rose bushes, which were wilting in the summer heat. She pounded her fist against the barrier. Iridescent waves rippled outwards from where she struck it.

"Now what are we going to do?"

Her book bag grew warmer. She had a strange inkling that the book inside it was laughing, mocking her. She threw the bag in the dirt beside the flowers.

Timothy ran to catch up to her.

"Why don't you just blast the book? Use that spell you used yesterday."

Fable bit her lip. She hadn't meant to blast Duncan. She didn't know how she had done it. And the side effect of a floating Grimm hadn't been ideal either. How would the book react if she blasted it?

She stared at her bag in the dirt. Even now that she wasn't touching it, she could still feel the book taunting her. She fiddled with the hem of her dress and tugged at some loose threads as she mulled it over. Would her magic trigger the nightmare, making it come alive again? But she didn't have any better ideas.

"Okay. I guess it's all we've got."

Timothy punched the air. "It'll work, I know it! You blasted Duncan right off the trail. Imagine what that'll do to a book." He grinned in anticipation.

Fable picked up the bag and brought it over to the maple tree. She took the book out of the bag and propped it up against the trunk. A white-hot wave of energy rolled off of it, and the vines whipped violently back and forth across its cover.

"Well, do it." Timothy stood a few feet behind her, off to the side of the tree, with Grimm beside him.

Fable swallowed her fear and walked ten paces away from the tree. She spun on her heel to face the book, which vibrated against the trunk. The belt

44

strained as the book struggled to break free.

It's just a book. Fable took a deep breath. *Nothing to be afraid of.*

She rubbed her hands together and a warm tingle built up between them. The book let out a horrible shriek, like brakes squealing, and Timothy covered his ears. She steeled herself against the screaming, sure that her ear-drums would burst it was so loud.

She slid her hands together until the tingle turned into a burn. She thought about how badly she wanted that horrible book to be gone and to be safe in her own bed at night. Her heart thumped in her chest and she pointed her palms at the book.

A huge ball of energy burst from her. It hurled through the air like a runaway freight train and hit the book with a loud CRACK.

The book jumped a foot into the air. The belt snapped and it landed open on the ground. The air around it rippled outwards, bending the grass and leaves. And then, everything became still.

Fable glanced at Timothy, who shrugged his shoulders and started walking towards the book.

"Well, that was disappointing." He squatted down to examine it. "I don't think—"

Dark purple-and-grey smoke poured out from the pages. Timothy's eyes widened in alarm as the cloud engulfed his body.

"Fable?"

Fable stood rooted to the ground, her heart beating wildly. "Timothy! Get out of there!"

A dark tendril shot out of the book and wrapped around Timothy's ankle. He flinched, then fell backwards out of the dense smoke onto his bottom and tried to scramble away. The tentacle held him fast, pulling him toward the gaping maw.

Fable sprinted towards him. Another tentacle reached out from the book and grabbed Timothy around the waist. She watched in horror as it dragged him towards the open pages.

She chased after him, desperately trying to conjure magic. Sparks shot from her fingers, but they fizzled and snuffed out. The tentacles wrapped around more of Timothy's body, dragging him across the lawn at alarming speed. He dug his fingers into the earth, scrambling for something to hold onto.

"Fable!"

Fable screamed and fell to her knees, grabbing Timothy's hands. Black smoke poured from the book, blinding her. His fingers slid from her grip. She watched helplessly as he disappeared from her sight.

The book still lay open, smoke billowing in every

direction. A dark funnel cloud appeared in the smoke. Without thinking, she dove into the book after him.

The book slammed shut, folding itself inside-out and down through the smoky hole behind the girl. The smoke melted away and was gone.

A panicking, snarling Grimm dove to follow his children.

He hit the ground with a loud crunch. He snorted and snuffled, foam pouring from his jowls as he searched for them. He wriggled behind the tree, under the rose bushes, and inside the garden shed. He let out a small whine. The sweet smell of syrup from their breakfast lingered in the air, but his children didn't seem to be anywhere.

In despair, he sat down and howled.

The Burntwood Forest

Fable noticed the trees first. Tall black trees with sooty branches that held no needles. Their bark peeled off in papery, ashen flakes. A flicker of fear rose in her chest. Fire. Burned out now, but one had been through here recently.

Laying on her back on the forest floor, she squinted in the bright sunlight. Her entire body ached. With a loud moan, she eased herself upright.

Suddenly, the memory of Timothy being pulled into the book and jumping in after him hit her. She scrambled to her feet and called out.

"Timothy!"

Frantically, she searched the clearing. She looked behind fallen, burnt logs, continuing to call his name.

"Timothy! Where are you?"

He was nowhere in sight. No Timothy, and no friendly black-nosed Grimm to soothe her. Her gaze rested on the book that lay on the ground near where she had awoken. That horrible, evil book—or the

48

Book of Chaos, as Timothy had named it—that stole her away here to . . . wherever she was. The book that kidnapped her cousin. It lay in the dirt, looking and acting like a normal book should.

Fable stared at the book, eyeing it warily. Gingerly, she reached out her foot and nudged it with her toe. The book slid sideways through the dirt but gave no reaction. She picked it up. It was cool to the touch, no trace of heat or smoldering fire. She flipped through the wrinkled, warped pages. It was still blank. The only markings were the scorched burn marks and grimy smudges.

Her heart sank. The book held no clues as to where she was. Or where Timothy was, either.

She squeezed her eyes shut and breathed deeply to calm her racing heart. When her fear subsided, she opened them and took stock of the situation. The forest was unfamiliar. Besides, there had been no fires near Larkmoor in years.

Her dress was filthy, streaked black with soot and dirt. Dried grass and leaves were entwined in her hair. She drew in a slow, deliberate breath.

"Umm, dear?" The voice came from behind her. "Is this your bag?"

Fable whirled around. A hen perched on her bag,

which lay on the ground at her feet. It was a plain-looking bird, her plumage a mottled brown with moss-coloured spots. A small leather pouch hung around her neck. She looked at Fable with long dark eyelashes and gave a quiet cluck as though she were clearing her throat.

"Dear?" Her beak opened and closed while the word was spoken, and it sounded like it came from the bird.

Chickens don't talk. Fable looked around. "Who said that?"

The hen cocked her head to one side. "What do you mean, 'who said that'? I'm right here."

Fable looked down at her. "That's not possible."

The hen ruffled her feathers. She had a look of annoyance on her face, which is a very strange look for a bird to have.

"Well, I suppose you must be right. Good luck finding whoever it is who has been speaking to you. While you're doing that, I'm going to work at getting these shiny things unstuck."

She pecked and bit at one of the silver stars on Fable's bag.

"Stop it." Fable marched over to the bag. "That's my bag! You're wrecking it."

"Be sure to tell that to the person who's been speaking to you." The hen ripped up a point of one of the star patches. With a squawk, she latched onto it with her beak and pulled harder.

"I said 'stop!'" Fable picked up her bag by its strap, but the talking hen held on to the star patch and yanked on it with surprising force.

"Hey!" Fable jerked at the strap, and the star patch ripped off completely. The bird toppled over backwards and flapped to her feet triumphantly, the torn-off star patch hanging from her beak.

"You little devil! You wrecked my bag."

Fable sat down in the dirt and fought back tears. Here she was, lost in a strange forest with a talking hen. She put the book down, sitting on it just in case it decided to go off, and hugged her bag. A dark blue star shape marked where the patch had been. A tear slid slowly down her cheek. She glared at the hen.

The hen smoothed her feathers, extended her neck and gazed at the crying girl from one golden eye. After placing the patch gently on the ground, the round bird pattered up to her.

"Little girl, what's wrong?" The hen peered up under the curtain of dark hair hiding Fable's face. "You can keep the shiny thing if you really want."

Jessica Renwick

Fable's face softened and she wiped away the tear.

"It's not just that," she said. "I'm lost, and my cousin is gone. I don't know where to even look. Or how to get home."

"Where's your home?" The precocious hen clambered into Fable's lap.

Fable set the book bag beside them on the ground.

"Larkmoor, in Starfell."

"We're in Starfell, but I've never heard of Larkmoor. I'm sure the Fey Witch would help you."

"The Fey Witch?"

"Yes. The Fey Witch knows everything and has been everywhere." The bird bobbed her head. "A few years ago, a band of weasels stole my flock's eggs, close to their hatch date. One of our members stumbled upon the Fey Witch on the trail. He told our story, and the Fey Witch unleashed a fury on those weasel bandits. Our eggs were returned well before the chicks arrived. I never met the witch myself, but I wish I could have."

"She sounds powerful. How can I find her?"

"Your best bet would be to find the Fey Witch's cottage."

"Can you help me find it?" Fable asked.

"It is said to be deep in the Lichwood Forest." The hen cocked her head in thought. "We Firehawks are not

52

safe in there. But I'll take you to the edge of it."

"We're not in the Lichwood Forest?"

"No, we're in the Burntwood Forest, dear." The Firehawk hopped off her lap and stepped back over to the silver star emblem where it lay on the ground. She picked it up and brought it back to Fable, her neck stretched out in offering.

Fable smiled, sniffling. "You keep it."

The bird flapped her wings and made a happy clucking sound deep in her throat. "Thank you! It's so shiny. My flock will be most impressed." She tucked her head down and placed the star patch safely in the pouch around her neck.

Fable stood up and slung her book bag over her shoulder. She gave the *Book of Chaos* another prod with her toe. It didn't react.

"What's that?" the hen asked.

"A book that tried to kill me."

The bird looked at it sideways. "That's impossible. Books aren't alive."

"You sound like my aunt." Fable picked up the book and tucked it into her bag.

"Why?"

"Never mind."

They walked side by side through the blackened

trees. Having a companion eased Fable's fear—even if that companion was a farmyard bird.

"What's your name?" Fable asked.

"Firehawks don't have names," the Firehawk replied. "Names are only for you tall folks. We tell each other apart by our auras and can sense our kind from miles away. In fact, my flock is about half a mile up this trail, hunting."

"Auras?" That sounded a bit far-fetched to Fable. Then again, she did just fly through a book and was currently speaking to a chicken. She glanced down at her new friend.

"Yes. You know . . . the feelings and senses that roll off a being." The Firehawk nodded. "In my flock there's the one whose aura makes you feel giggly and smells like cotton candy. Then there's the one who makes you feel at peace, with a soft breeze on your face and the smell of fresh grass."

She seemed to be lost in thought. "Of course, not all are so lovely. There's also the one whose aura stinks like rotten eggs. I try to stay away from him."

Fable tried to imagine her new friend's flock.

"A being's aura reflects who they are inside." The Firehawk hopped over a fallen tree. "It's really quite useful. I can tell right away if somebody is good, or if

54

I should stay away from them."

"Can you sense my aura?" Fable asked.

The little bird stopped and Fable stood next to her. She looked at Fable with pretty, dark eyes. "A little bit of chaos, like a rolling storm with bits of electricity sparking about." She paused. "There's some sweetness there too. Like wild bramble berries on a hot summer day. I like it."

Fable pondered on the Firehawk's words. She wondered what Timothy's aura would be. And Grimm's, and Aunt Moira's. Her gut clenched at the thought of her family.

"And what is your name?" the bird asked her as they continued down the trail.

"Fable."

"That's pretty. Is it a family name?" the bird asked they walked around a wall of dirty roots from a fallen tree.

Before Fable could answer, the Firehawk flapped her wings and jumped a foot into the air. She opened her beak and a three-foot flame burst from her mouth, singeing the ferns alongside the trail. Fable's jaw fell open and she stared. As quickly as it had begun, the spurt petered out.

Firehawk. Of course. The squat bird was more

dangerous than she appeared.

The hen gulped for fresh air and squatted down to the ground. With a little squawk, she stood up and a fiery orange egg lay on the ground underneath her.

"Oh my, not again." The bird stamped her feet. She leaned down and nuzzled the egg.

"I'm so embarrassed. This always happens at the worst time." She used the underside of her beak to nudge the egg into her pouch, where she'd hidden the silver star. "I am so sorry you had to see that."

Fable waved her hand in front of her face and coughed. When the smoke cleared, she looked up and saw why the bird had panicked.

A girl the size of a full-grown man sat cross-legged beside a fallen tree. Fable took a few steps back and fumbled with her bag, accidentally grabbing it by the bottom and turning it upside-down. The book slipped out and fell to the ground.

The girl looked young, around Fable's age or maybe a year older, but Fable had never seen anyone like her. Underneath the sparse grey hair on her arms and legs, her skin was a bluish grey, and she had pointed ears that stuck out from her long copper hair. Her heavily-matted mane hung down past her waist, with feathers and beads braided into random sections throughout it.

She wore a crude knee-length burlap dress that looked like the pieces had been hacked out of the fabric with a butter knife. Smoke curled up from the jagged hem.

The giant girl patted out an orange flame by her knee and then stared directly at the Firehawk with piercing green eyes.

She closed them and took a deep breath. After counting to five, she opened them. "Umm. I'm trying to meditate here. Would you mind taking your fiery breath somewhere else?"

Fable eyed the double-headed ax leaning against the tree behind the girl. It was massive, at least as tall as Fable herself. Sunlight glinted off the sharp edges.

Her Firehawk friend spoke to the girl. "I am so sorry, miss . . .—er, ma'am . . .— er, beast?"

"Thorn."

"Thorn?"

"My name is Thorn."

The bird cocked her head. "Oh. Hello, Thorn."

Thorn looked at her but said nothing. She rested her hands on her knees, grey palms facing up.

"You just surprised us, that's all," the Firehawk said. "Again, my apologies. Fable and I will be on our way."

Fable bent down and picked up her dirt-smeared book. She wiped it off with her hand and was about to put it back into her bag when Thorn spoke.

"What's that?"

"A book."

"What kind of book?" Thorn stared it with curiosity.

"I'm not sure. It's blank inside." Fable held it close to her chest.

"I know that pattern," Thorn said. "My sister's an archer. She has a bow with vines just like those ones painted on it." She pointed a finger towards the cover.

"Your sister? Where is she?" Fable asked.

Thorn shook her head and dropped her hand. "I don't know. A few weeks ago, when the fire swept through, everybody in our colony had to flee. I got separated from my family."

"I'm sorry. I know how you feel. I've lost my family, too."

"Oh. I'm sorry, too." There was a note of sadness in Thorn's voice. "You're not from around here." She blinked at Fable's yellow dress.

"I'm from Larkmoor."

"How'd you get all the way out here?"

"You've heard of Larkmoor?" A spark of hope lit up inside Fable.

Thorn nodded, her wild hair flying around her face. "Yeah. It's a long way from here. Over the mountains, past the Lichwood Forest."

Fable's face fell. She could just make out the tops of the mountains, far off in the distance. "Really?"

"You'll be well on your way once you reach the Lichwood," the Firehawk said. "Speaking of which, it's going to be dark soon. We should go."

"The Lichwood? You won't make it there before dark." Thorn looked up at the sky. Dusk had begun to set, cloaking the world in soft blue light.

"You can camp with me if you want. I'm heading to the Lichwood myself to see the Fey Witch." Thorn glanced down at Fable, her face half-hidden behind her tangled mane. "We could travel together."

"The Fey Witch?" Fable asked. "That's where I'm going, too. I hope she can help me."

Thorn nodded. "If anybody can help you, it's the Fey Witch. My dad once told me about a boy from our colony who got swept downstream while he was catching minnows. He was missing for several days. His dad walked for two days to the Fey Witch's cottage and asked for help, and the next morning the boy's mom found him sleeping in his bed."

"That's amazing!"

59

The Firehawk cocked her head and with one eye peered up at the girl. "Do you have a warm place to sleep?"

Thorn grinned and jerked her head to the side. Fable peered around her into a small clearing. There was a fire pit, already filled with moss and twigs, ready to be lit. A green tent, big enough that Thorn's feet wouldn't stick out the end, stood pegged under a tree.

"I've been here a few days now, resting." Thorn unfolded her bulky frame, towering over them as she rose. She smoothed out her wrinkly burlap dress, then stepped over and picked up the ax. Despite its massive size, Thorn swung it easily over her shoulder. She led the way to her camp site. "Are you hungry?"

"We don't need to bother you for food. There's a tavern on the way to the Lichwood for Fable, and I can find supper on the way." The Firehawk had to flutter and do a funny little hop-skip to keep up with the giant girl's long strides.

"I don't have the money for that." Thorn shook her head. "I'm just a Folkvar. We live off the land."

"A Folkvar?" Fable jogged to keep up.

"Yes, a Greenwood Folkvar."

"Greenwood? Where is that?"

Thorn looked down at her. "Here. Before the fire

came through and turned it into the Burntwood."

"Oh." Fable replied. *Obviously.*

They reached the sturdy green canvas tent. It would have blended into the forest before the fire. Now, it stood out in stark contrast with the sooty bark of the trees around it.

Thorn pulled back the flap of the door. Inside was a green sleeping bag, a canvas backpack, a cast iron pan, and a pile of brown mushrooms. The gear all looked just like any other camper's gear would, except everything was enormous.

"You've been foraging." The Firehawk eyed the pile of mushrooms and clucked.

"Morels." Thorn licked her lips. "Delicious little fungi. My dad taught me how to forage. These brown ones, if you slice open the caps and they're hollow, then they're safe to eat. If they're solid, you'd better toss 'em back."

"What happens if you eat the solid ones?" Fable asked.

"I don't think you'd survive to find out."

The air had taken on a sharp, frosty bite as the sky had darkened. Fable rubbed her arms, her skin pebbled like a Harvest Day turkey, ready for the oven. Her stomach growled at the thought of food and she cast a guilty glance at the Firehawk.

"Cold?" Thorn rummaged through the tent. "I have a sweater in here somewhere. I don't need it unless it gets below freezing—all this hair." She motioned to the hair on her arm. "Aha!"

She stood up with a knitted moss-green wool sweater the size of a blanket in her hands. It was stiff with filth. Thorn handed it to Fable.

Fable sniffed it, and the smell of stale woodsmoke filled her nostrils. It didn't matter. They were camping, and she was cold. She pulled it over her head. It hung well past her knees, but she appreciated the warmth.

"Thanks." Fable smiled at her.

Thorn eyed her, then began filling the pan with mushrooms. "You're not really prepared for the wild."

Fable shrugged her shoulders. "This was kind of an unexpected trip."

Dirt and Muskeg

Fable woke to the sound of a crackling fire and voices outside the tent. She crawled to the door and peered outside. Thorn, her copper hair looking even wilder than the night before, sat on a stump facing the fire with her back to the tent. The Firehawk perched on a log beside her, looking like a tiny songbird next to the towering Folkvar girl.

"Can your kind read auras too?" the Firehawk asked.

Thorn snorted. "Auras? What kind of mumbo-jumbo is that?"

Mushrooms sizzled and popped in the frying pan over the fire. Thorn picked up her wooden spoon and gave them a stir.

The Firehawk fluffed up her brown feathers. "Mumbo-jumbo? I think not. We can see everybody's aura. Including yours."

"And what's mine?"

"Dirt, muskeg, and muddy river water."

63

Thorn flicked a mushroom at the bird with her spoon. The Firehawk ducked out of the way, and it flew into the bushes behind her.

"Good morning." Fable climbed out of the tent. "That smells delicious."

"Morning," Thorn replied.

The Firehawk perked up at the sight of her new friend. "Good morning, Fable," she sang.

Fable joined them in front of the fire. Thorn's tangled locks hung down over her face as she stirred their breakfast. Fable combed at hers with her fingers, wishing she had a brush.

The Firehawk tutted and chirped as she preened at her feathers on the log.

Gazing fondly at the bird, Fable decided she deserved to be called something nicer than "the Firehawk."

"I know, Miss Firehawk, that you don't use names," she said. "But I think it'd be easier for me if I could give you a nickname. Would you like that?"

"A nickname?" The bird cocked her head to the side.

"You know, a name your friends call you. A name of affection."

Thorn gave a mischievous smile. "Bird Brain?"

The Firehawk squawked, flapped her wings, and

shot the giant girl a dirty look.

Fable stifled a smile. "Something nicer than that."

"Well, I suppose that could be fun," the bird said. "I've never had a name before. Can I pick it?"

"You don't usually get to pick your nickname. But if you really want to, sure."

The Firehawk reached into the pouch around her neck and re-emerged with the silver star hanging from her beak. She placed it carefully down on the log at her feet. Her chest feathers ruffled and fluffed.

"I would like to be called Star."

Thorn snorted.

Star glared at her. "It's certainly better than *Thorn*!"

Fable grinned and stroked Star's back. "It suits you perfectly. Star it is."

Star warbled and closed her eyes while Fable petted her. When Fable pulled her hand away, Star tucked her shiny treasure back into her pouch.

Thorn stood up and removed the pan from the fire.

"Move it over, *Star*."

Star hopped quickly out of the way, and Thorn placed the pan down in her spot.

"Mushrooms again. They're all I've been able to find around here, what with the fire and all."

"They're perfect. Thank you." Fable's stomach rumbled as the delicious, savoury odour of crisp golden mushrooms wafted up to her.

Star eyed the food and sniffed. "I'm going to see if I can scrounge up some shade beetles. I won't be far."

She hopped off her stump and strutted into the trees.

Thorn sat on the other side of the pan, her burlap dress straining as she straddled the log. She handed Fable a roughly carved wooden spoon. She'd made it herself, she'd explained with pride the evening before. Another skill taught to her by her woodsman father.

Fable took a scoop of the buttery, earthy mushrooms and closed her eyes as she chewed. It felt like she hadn't eaten in days. As she gobbled up the breakfast, she thought about the bow Thorn had mentioned the day before, the one with the same vine pattern as her book. They had to be related. She wondered if it came from the same place and had the same dark magic.

"Umm, Thorn?" she asked between bites.

Thorn looked up from the meal. A mushroom fell from her spoon into the long hair that hung over her shoulder. She picked it out with her fingers and popped it into her mouth.

"Your sister's bow. Did it do anything strange?"

"I dunno. Orchid said it would never miss." Thorn wiped her mouth with the back of her hand. "She bought it from some old lady right before the fire. The

66

woman said it was magic, that it always hit its mark. No idea if it was true, though. I never got to see her use it."

That wasn't a strange claim to make when one was trying to sell a magical weapon. And it certainly wasn't the odd behaviour Fable had in mind. At least nothing like tentacles, smoke and kidnapping.

"Does your book do anything weird?" Thorn asked.

Fable thought about the book that lay innocently in her bag in the tent. She licked the wooden spoon and set it down in the pan.

"It depends on what you think is weird, I guess."

Thorn chewed slowly, gazing thoughtfully at Fable. "Well, I think that a book doing anything un-book-like would be weird."

"Un-book-like?" Fable shifted her seat.

"You know, like drawing its own pictures. Or ruining the ending of its own story." Thorn paused, rough wooden spoon halfway to her mouth. "Or zap its reader into another world."

Fable's hands grew clammy. Suddenly, the sweater she wore was far too hot.

Thorn slapped her knee. Mushrooms fell from her spoon. Her booming laugh rang through the trees.

"It's rare, but I heard that it happened in Mistford once. A long time ago, to a librarian. The poor guy was reading about Firecrest dragons, and he was transported right into Halite's lair."

"Halite?"

"You don't know who Halite is? The dragon queen." Thorn gulped down what was left of her spoonful of breakfast. "The fiercest Firecrest dragon in all of Starfell. Anyways, I'm not sure if it's true. It's a story my sister told me."

"Oh." *Dragons?* "Well, no, my book hasn't transported anyone into a dragon's den." Not that she knew of anyways. "It's blank. No words, or pictures, or anything." Despite the buttery mushrooms, her mouth felt dry. What would this strange girl think if Fable told her about the book portal? *About how I let it take Timothy?*

"Really?" Thorn asked. "What good is a book with no stories?"

Avoiding Thorn's gaze, Fable shrugged her shoulders. "Not a very good one."

After finishing breakfast, they packed up camp. Thorn soon had the tent and sleeping bag rolled up into her backpack.

Fable stood up on a tree stump to tie the frying pan to the outside of the pack. "Why don't you want the pan inside with everything else?"

"I like to have it handy," Thorn said. "It packs a

pretty hard hit. Perfect when I need another weapon."

Thorn picked up the ax that stood up to her chin. It seemed like that should be weapon enough.

Fable slung her book bag over her shoulder. The knot in the tie caught on the large knit sweater she was still wearing. She untangled it carefully and thought about what she had gotten herself into. *If a giant Folkvar girl needs an ax like that, what about someone my size?* She didn't have any weapons. No protection. She stepped closer to Thorn.

This world outside of Larkmoor was so different. Fable had never heard anybody talk so freely of weapons, or of creatures like dragons.

"Thorn, how do you know about Larkmoor? I've never heard of Folkvars. Or Firehawks. Or the Burntwood Forest, or any of the places you and Star have talked about."

Thorn shrugged her shoulders. "I've never been there, but people talk about it. It was settled a few hundred years ago. There were a few human families who feared magic and the other races here. They decided to cross the Windswept Mountains and set up their own village, cut off from the rest Starfell."

"Oh," Fable said. This was news to her, but it made sense. At school, they never learned about the other people or cities in Starfell. Their geography classes never went beyond the mountain range that cut them off from the world. Fable only knew of Mistford, the city her family was from, because of the few stories of her parents that Aunt Moira had told her.

Star returned from her bug hunt.

"Full?" Fable asked.

Star bobbed her head. "I found a ton of dew worms in the bushes behind the tent."

"Gross." Thorn frowned, then turned to Fable. "Ready?"

"Lead the way."

The trio started down the worn path towards the mountains in the distance.

NINE

Buttertub Tavern

After several hours of walking, the path they were on crossed over a wide dirt road. They stopped at the crossroads to rest. Behind them lay the blackened trees of the Burntwood Forest. Across the road, the pine trees stood green and full.

The path on that side lay in darkness under a thick canopy of branches and needles. A craggy wooden sign was nailed to a tree where the path entered the forest. It read "Lichwood Forest" in crude, red-painted letters.

Thorn leaned her ax against a nearby tree and dropped her backpack to the ground. "This is the Parting of the Forests," she said, gesturing at the boundary road.

Star let out a cluck of exhaustion and sank down into a puddle of feathers at Fable's feet. "It is high time we had a rest." She began pecking the ground around her in search of bugs.

Thorn spread her feet wide and bent forward at the

71

waist with her arms perpendicular to her body until her hands reached the ground. Fable recognized the stretch as a yoga position called the "forward fold".

Every morning, Aunt Moira did a yoga routine in the garden. She said both her body and mind needed the stretching to prepare for a day's work, whatever that meant. The petunias always had a better bloom after Moira practiced her yoga with them. Fable smiled, thinking about her aunt doing headstands for the flowers.

"This road leads to Stonebarrow in the North and to Mistford in the south." Thorn turned and raised her arms, then lowered herself into the warrior pose. "If we head up the road a bit, the Buttertub Tavern is just around the bend."

Fable's stomach rumbled, her mushroom breakfast long since digested. "Do they have food?"

"Do you have money for food?"

"No." Fable thought wistfully of her piggy bank back at Rose Cottage. What she would give for a burger and some fries swimming in gravy. With fresh lemonade to wash it all down.

Thorn, legs still spread wide in warrior pose, patted the rough pocket sewn crudely on the front of her dress. She pulled out a turnip and tossed it to Fable.

Fable caught it with both hands. She examined it

carefully and picked off bits of fibre before taking a bite. It didn't quite match up to that burger in her mind, but it was better than nothing.

"Thanks," she said, slowly chewing the tough vegetable. It still tasted like the soil it had been pulled from.

Thorn nodded a welcome as she shifted poses again, raising her arms above her head.

Star smacked her beak, apparently satisfied from her bug hunt. "I'm not sure if it's worth anything, but I found this a few days ago on the trail."

She ducked her beak into her pouch, and after some shuffling and a few high-pitched chirps, she re-emerged with a shiny gold coin in her beak.

Thorn raised her eye brows. "You found that?" She switched into another pose, standing up straight with her palms together in front of her. "That's enough to buy both Fable and I a good lunch, with change to spare."

Star stepped away from Thorn and shot her a disgruntled look. She stretched out her neck and offered the coin to Fable.

Fable carefully took it from her. "Thank you, Star. Are you sure?"

"You let me keep that shiny badge from your bag." Star cocked her head. "Fair trade, I think?"

"I'll pay you back later." Fable smiled. Her stomach growled loudly at the thought of the hamburger waiting for her at the tavern.

Thorn shook out her whole body, and after one last stretch, she put on her backpack and picked up her ax.

The three made their way down the Parting Road. They rounded a bend, and to Fable's delight, a little restaurant popped into view in a clearing on the Lichwood side. The small stone building had a chimney that puffed smoke into the air and a large sign above the door that read "Buttertub Tavern—Food and Drink for the weary traveler".

The parking area in the front was full of clunky, old cars. Two hogs in the back of a rusty red truck pressed their snouts through the bars of their pen and snuffled at the group as they approached. Fable reached up to pat one, and it squealed and shied away from her hand.

When they reached the door, Star glanced at the small chalkboard sign beside it. A smiling sketch of a hen grinned out at them above the words "Daily Special—Roast Chicken".

"I'm going to wait outside and search for bugs." With a sniff, she wandered off towards the edge of the woods.

"Are we allowed inside?" Fable asked.

"Why wouldn't we be?" Thorn lifted her arm and

gave herself a sniff. "Do I smell that bad? I can't tell after a few days in woods. My nose gets used to it."

"No, it's just children aren't allowed inside pubs in Larkmoor."

"That doesn't seem fair. What's wrong with children?" Thorn pushed open the door of the tavern and ducked her head below the jamb as they entered.

They stood there, letting their eyes adjust to the dim lighting. Several long tables in front of a bar hosted patrons of all shapes and sizes, some drinking from frosted mugs and some with plates piled high with food in front of them.

A rack beside the door overflowed with swords, axes, and thick wooden clubs beneath a sign in big bold letters that stated that all weapons were to be left there. The fine letters underneath said they had a zero-tolerance policy on "rolling heads" inside the tavern. Fable wondered if they were serious.

Thorn placed her ax on the rack and nudged Fable. "I've still got the frying pan. Just in case."

Fable blinked back at her, disconcerted.

Thorn pointed across the room. "There's two spots."

The barkeep—a short portly fellow with more hair on his face than on top of his head—eyed Thorn's towering figure and wild hair as they edged along the bar, his eyebrows climbing to his non-existent hairline. Thorn cast him a sharp glance and he ducked his head, pointedly engrossed in pouring a drink for the red-nosed man with watery eyes who was perched at the bar in front of him.

The customer hiccupped, oblivious to the young Folkvar behind him. "A little more, Murphy! I've—hic—had a hard—hic—day."

Thorn pushed her way through a loud group of men with pint-sized mugs of ale. Her backpack bounced off several heads as she forced her way through the crowd. The patrons shouted in surprise, throwing angry looks in her direction. Without any sign that she'd noticed, Thorn continued down the line toward the open seats.

Fable slipped through behind her. "I'm really sorry. I don't think she knows how big she is. She doesn't mean it."

The customers mumbled and glared, but nobody moved from their seats.

Thorn plunked herself down at the end of the table with a loud thud. The other end of the bench popped up into the air, unseating a small man about Fable's size.

"Hey!" He glared at the giant of a girl and struggled to scramble back onto his seat. Thorn ignored him. He sighed and moved to another table, glowering at her over his shoulder.

Thorn stood up, shrugged off her backpack and placed it on the seat where the little man had sat moments before. Fable sat down next to her.

A rather round woman with grey hair and a grungy apron approached them with a pad of paper and a pencil. With her wrestler's forearms and scarred face, she looked like she'd settled her fair share of tavern brawls.

"What will it be?" Her voice sounded like tires crunching on gravel. She passed Thorn a worn menu.

Thorn gazed at it for a moment. "Roasted root vegetables and gravy, beans with molasses but no pork, vegetable soup, curried rice, a peanut butter sandwich, and a garden salad with dressing on the side. Please." She snapped the menu shut and placed it on the table.

The waitress scribbled down the order. "No special?"

"I'm a vegetarian," Thorn replied.

"Oh, right. Sorry, I forgot your kind don't eat flesh." The waitress looked down at Fable. "And you, little miss?"

"Just a hamburger and fries, please."

The waitress gave her a curt nod, collected Thorn's menu, and hastened toward the kitchen.

Fable looked around, taking in the tavern scene.

She'd never been anywhere like this before. At the

front of the room, a short stout woman crooned a love song, backed by a tall thin man playing the guitar with his eyes closed. The singer's long skirt swayed in time with the song. She reminded Fable of Aunt Moira.

The outside world was so different from Larkmoor. She and Thorn would be quite the unusual pair at home. Fable, looking like a street urchin in her oversized, smelly sweater, and Thorn, a giant grey Folkvar girl, larger than most men. Here, the only attention they received was for Thorn's impression of a bull in a china shop. Now that they were seated and the other patrons' heads were safe from Thorn's backpack, all backs were turned and the tavern buzzed with the sounds of talking and laughter.

The waitress returned with three teenage boys carrying Thorn's food. After the servers had placed dish after dish in front of them, Fable handed the waitress the gold coin. The woman put it in the pocket of her dirty apron and fished out a few smaller silver coins in return.

"Anything else I can get for you girls?"

"I think we're good." Thorn had a huge grin on her face as she ogled all the food before her.

A surly-faced bald man thumped his fist on the table behind them. "Hilda! More ale!"

"Hold your horses," the waitress shouted back at

him. With a tight smile at the girls, she and her helpers hurried away.

Fable placed the coins on the table in front of her and admired the flying dragons imprinted on them. She'd never seen coins like this before. Beautiful and shiny, the dragons glistened in the dim light around them.

She dug into her fries. Her stomach had been aching with hunger and the food was delicious, warm, and satisfying. Thorn ate her vegetarian meal with ferocious enthusiasm.

"I haven't had a real meal in so long." Her beans disappeared in three large bites. She pushed the bowl away and let out a large belch in appreciation.

Once the girls finished their meal, Fable patted her belly, feeling full and content.

"I'll be right back." Thorn stood up. "I need to use the throne." She plowed her way through the tight walkway between the tables.

"Hey!" a bearded man shouted, jumping to his feet as his ale spilled onto his lap.

She kept going.

Fable rested her chin in her hands and listened to the music. This was the most content she'd felt since she fell through the book. Her thoughts wandered to Timothy, and her face grew hot as guilt washed over her. How could she allow herself to be so content when her cousin was still missing? She should be out there searching for him, not enjoying a warm meal and a concert. It was her fault he was gone. He could be scared and alone right now. Or worse.

A deep voice behind her interrupted her thoughts. "Hodgkins has been missing for three days now. No sign of him, not a trace."

Fable peeked over her shoulder and saw a tall, broad man with his head bent talking to a slight man who looked like he had just come from working in a farmer's field.

The second man pulled at the collar of his dirt-stained shirt. "Frank's wife disappeared a few weeks ago. Same thing, no evidence. I figured she'd just run off, what with Frank being, well, Frank. But this seems pretty fishy."

"Something strange is afoot." The broad man shook his head and took a sip of his ale. "There haven't been disappearances like this since Endora was loose in the forest."

Somebody bumped into Fable's table, jerking her attention away from the conversation. She glanced over to see a boy, probably thirteen or fourteen years old, land on his rump behind her.

"Oh, hey! Are you okay?" She offered him a hand.

He took it and she helped him to his feet.

"Gosh, I'm so sorry, miss!" He brushed the dust off his jeans and black hooded sweatshirt. He was taller than Fable, with russet brown skin, black hair, and a thin build. "I'm such a klutz, tripping over my own two feet like that. I hope I didn't hurt you."

"I'm fine." She noticed a red mark on his hand where he had skinned it. "Here, sit down. We should clean that up."

The boy smiled and straddled the bench next to her. She took his hand and turned it palm up in her own. She glanced up to find him watching her with warm brown eyes. Heat crept up over her cheeks.

After dipping her napkin into her water glass, she used it to dab at his bleeding palm. Her hands warmed, and new, healthy pink skin grew over the spot where his wound had been just a few seconds before. She gazed at his palm. She'd never done anything like that before.

"How'd you do that?" He asked. He held out his palm in front of his face. "Amazing. Pretty, and a healer as well." He winked.

Fable blushed. She ran her hands over her hair (which hadn't been washed since she was back at Rose Cottage), trying to smooth the tangles.

"Um . . . thanks," she said. "What's your name?"

The boy stood up and looked towards the bar. "Sorry, I hear my father calling. Was nice meeting you."

He left as suddenly as he'd arrived.

Fable shrugged. She played with her hair, still beaming from the compliment. Nobody had ever told her she was pretty before. She was beginning to like it out here in the real world of Starfell—outside of the drab, boring Larkmoor. People were kinder, and a lot more interesting.

Thorn arrived back at the table, leaving a trail of thumps and disgruntled comments behind her. She picked up her backpack and heaved it over her shoulders.

"Ready? We better go find Star before she's mistaken for dinner."

Fable nodded and stood up from her seat. She gathered her bag.

"Where's your change?" Thorn asked.

"What?"

"Your change. From the waitress."

Fable looked down at the table, a sinking feeling in her chest. The coins were gone.

Thieves and Morals

"Your coins. They were right there. Did you put them in your bag?"

Fable's breath caught. She moved her dirty plate in search of the money. The table was bare. "I—I don't know."

Thorn set her mouth in a firm line. "Did anybody walk by here while I was gone? I forgot you're not from here. I should've warned you. Thieves love taverns."

Fable's heart fell to her stomach. *Of course.* Humiliation washed over her. How could she fall for such a trick? She'd been so happy that somebody found her appealing, but it had just been a ruse.

A lump in her throat, she scanned the tavern and saw the boy near the bar. He caught sight of her pointing at him and his eyes widened. He started to push his way through the crowd towards the exit.

"Stop!" Fable cried out. "Stop that boy."

Nobody heard her. She soon lost sight of him through the crowd of bodies.

"Stop!" Thorn bellowed.

She slammed a fist down onto the table next to her. The crowd fell silent. Even the performers stopped playing. All eyes were on Thorn.

Fable saw the back of the boy's shirt through the crowd. She pointed. "There he is."

"That boy stole my friend's money." Thorn pushed her way towards the exit, her face twisted in rage. She upended a whole table, and food and dishes flew through the air. The patrons turned their heads and stared at the boy, who had a look of terror on his face.

Two men wearing leather armour over green uniforms barred the exit. One grabbed his arms. Thorn stalked towards them.

Fable scampered along behind her. "Excuse me, I'm sorry about your food," she stammered to deaf ears as she passed.

Thorn caught up to the boy and grabbed the shoulder of his sweatshirt. Despite being around the same age, Thorn was a good foot taller than him and much broader. The guard let go of his arms, smirking, and Thorn pulled the boy's face to meet hers.

"Where's her money?"

"It's here. Right here. I didn't mean to . . ." He reached into his pocket and held out the coins.

"You didn't mean to steal from a little girl?" Thorn

asked through gritted teeth.

Fable wanted to object. Despite being small for her age, she *was* twelve years old, far from a little child. She pushed the thought away when she saw Thorn's red face. Her friend's eyes morphed from green to yellow.

One of the guards laid a hand on Thorn's arm. "We'll take him from here—er—miss?"

Thorn snatched the coins from the boy's outstretched palm with her free hand and let go of his sweater. He stumbled into the guards.

Thorn grabbed her ax from the weapons rack and stalked outside. Fable narrowed her eyes at the boy as she passed. His face paled and sweat shone from his forehead. The guards stood him up and tied his wrists behind his back. Maybe a few nights in jail would teach him a lesson about tricking girls and hurting their feelings.

It had started raining while they had been inside. Fable covered her head and ran and caught up to Thorn, who stood at edge of the clearing. Thorn's backpack lay in the mud at her feet, and her ax rested on her shoulder. The rain poured down her face onto the ground below.

"I need a few minutes." Thorn's eyes were still a weird shade of yellow, but the red slowly drained from her face.

"Okay," Fable said. "I'll find Star."

Thorn nodded and crashed into the bush out of Fable's sight.

Fable felt a small tug on her skirt. She looked down to find Star peering up at her. "What happened in there?"

"Some boy stole our change." Humiliated, she didn't want to tell the whole story. "Thorn stopped him, though. I got it back."

"I heard quite a commotion. Folkvars can be very convincing when they need to be. Are you okay?"

Other than my hurt pride?

"Yeah, I'm fine."

Fable sat down under the nearest tree to hide from the rain. The little Firehawk climbed into her lap.

"I'm glad you're okay," Star said. "Am I right in thinking that Larkmoor is a fair bit, shall we say, 'calmer' than here?"

"Yeah, you could say that."

"Don't worry, dear." Star nuzzled Fable's sweater. "That boy will have a much harder time stealing from anybody else."

"What do you mean?"

"Well, if the fear they put into him isn't enough, he'll only have one hand."

"What?" Fable bolted upright.

"That's the punishment for thievery. They'll cut off one of his hands." Star looked up at her, head turned to the side. "Probably the left one for a first-time offense. Don't worry, he'll still have the dominant one. Don't they do that in Larkmoor?"

"What? No! That's barbaric." Fable picked Star up with both hands and set her on the ground.

In Larkmoor, the most a petty thief would face was a few days behind bars to straighten him out. She'd read about punishments like this in books, but it had never crossed her mind that there were places in Starfell that actually resorted to such a brutal act. She felt sick to her stomach.

"He deserves it, Fable. He stole from you."

Despite his trick and Fable's hurt feelings, the thief was human. She closed her eyes as she thought of Timothy. What would she want a bystander to do if it were him in this boy's shoes? Her heart ached. What if he were in trouble like this?

Fable shook her head and got to her feet. Hands on her hips, she stared down at the bird.

"No. Nobody deserves that. We need to help him."

"If you say so. But I'm not sure if Thorn will be on board with it."

"We'll see about that." Fable sat back down under

the tree and crossed her arms.

Star stepped softly in front of her and pecked at her sleeve. With a sigh, Fable picked up the round little bird and placed her in her lap. Star turned three circles and snuggled herself down into Fable's warm sweater. The two sat together, hiding from the rain, waiting for Thorn to return.

"We can't let them do it," Fable said to Thorn's back.

Thorn adjusted the straps on her backpack and didn't turn around. "That's what happens to thieves. He knows that."

The rain had slowed down to a miserable mist. Just enough to keep Fable's sweater from drying out. It hung heavily around her shoulders.

"It's barbaric! You can't seriously think this is right."

"It doesn't matter what I think. Or what you think either." Thorn paused and turned around. She towered over Fable, her mouth set into a firm line.

"The guards won't to listen to us," she said. "That's the law. You steal, you lose your hand. You steal again, you lose your other hand. And if you're stupid enough to do it again . . ."

"He's a person. Just like us."

"He stole from you."

"So what?" Fable said. "In Larkmoor, thieves get jail time. We don't dismember them."

Thorn's nostrils flared as she let out a big breath. "It's different here. I don't like it either. In fact, I'd really like to get out of here before they do it."

"Leave?"

Clenching her jaw with determination, Fable marched up to Thorn and stood toe to toe with her. To the best of her ability, she craned her neck and looked Thorn square in the eye.

"Thorn, you know this isn't right. We're not leaving. We're helping him."

"What do you think we're going to do?" Thorn asked. Her face softened as she looked down at the small girl glowering up at her. "We can't just saunter up and ask them to let him go."

"I have a plan." Fable stood her ground, staring into the Folkvar's narrowed green eyes without flinching. "Trust me."

Thorn sighed, defeated, and dropped her backpack on the ground. "Fine. But I'm not risking my neck for him."

Proper Justice

F able and Thorn stood in front of the raised wooden platform behind the Buttertub Tavern. They had left Star to guard Thorn's ax in the trees near the opening of the path into the Lichwood. It was early afternoon, and while the rain had stopped, clouds still obscured the sky, casting the landscape into tones of dreary grey.

A crowd of people had gathered, excited by the promise of a show. The young thief, his hood up and hiding most of his face, stood on the platform with a guard on either side. A solid, heavy table stood in front of them.

The guards stood unmoving, their expressionless faces surveying the crowd. Each man held one of the prisoner's arms. There was no way he would be able to escape this alone.

"Heathen!" somebody from the crowd called out.

"Thief! He should be hanged!"

An apple bounced off the boy's head, and he flinched. One of the guards caught it and, with a grin at the crowd, took a bite. The crowd jeered with laughter, an angry mob hungry for entertainment. Fable grimaced when another apple was thrown at the stage.

"Are we really doing this?" Thorn didn't take her eyes off the scene before them.

Fable nodded.

Another guard approached the stage, followed by the portly bartender. Murphy now wore long navy-blue robes with a tinfoil badge on his chest. They climbed the stairs onto the stage, and Murphy took his position at the front of the platform.

Thorn rolled her eyes. "Oh, boy, here we go."

"What's with the badge?" Fable glanced up at her friend.

"The police never bother to drive all the way out here. Looks like Murphy has decided to take the law into his own hands."

Murphy puffed his chest out as he spoke and waved a hand towards the thief. "This boy here is charged with thievery. Stealing, inside the walls of my prestigious restaurant!"

He grew louder and more dramatic as he went on. "Great friends and patrons of the Buttertub, we all know the punishment for such a dastardly deed!"

The crowd hooted and cheered as Murphy waved

his arms theatrically in the air. The boy hung his head, his face hidden under the hood of his sweater.

"Get in position and wait for my signal," Fable said softly.

Thorn nodded. Fable worked her way slowly into the crowd.

Murphy called for witnesses to step forward. Fable crept through the patrons until she reached the corrals beside the tavern, near the rear of the mob. The pens housed a variety of farm animals standing quietly in the enclosures. None of the animals were paying attention to the commotion nearby. The horses swished their tails at flies as one nuzzled another's back. A Jersey cow chewed her cud, her soft eyelashes half closed.

Just as Fable took a step towards the gate, a burly man in a plaid jacket stumbled from the crowd and limped over to the corral. He sat on the ground and leaned his back against the fence, listening to Murphy bellow. After Murphy emoted with a particularly dramatic line, the man gave a loud hiccup and let out a slurred cheer.

Fable's heart dropped. What was she going to do now? She couldn't sneak over and open the gates as she had planned. Not with that man sitting there.

A thought snuck into her mind. Her hands tingled.

She tried to push the thought away. She wasn't prepared to use magic. Closing her eyes, Fable replayed the memory of the last time she had used magic, in the garden at Rose Cottage—when Timothy disappeared.

Witnesses lined up beside the stage, looking eager to tell their stories. The boy didn't move, his face still hidden beneath the hood of his sweatshirt. One of the guards was sharpening an ax. He scowled at the crowd and they goaded him on.

Panic seared through her. She had to act fast.

The drunken man flopped sideways, back still against the fence, and dropped his bottle to the ground. "I say hang him!" he shouted with a pump of his fist.

Fable glanced at the boy on the stage. He was trembling. She gritted her teeth and summoned every ounce of courage she had.

The corral gate was held shut with a simple wooden lever resting in a latch. Clearing her mind, she focused on it, and it began wiggling back and forth. But no matter how hard she rattled it, the lever didn't slide far enough to unhook. The movement caught a goat's attention. The doe perked up and stared at the jiggling lever, her ears alert.

Good girl. Fable stared at the goat, urging her on in her mind. One cloven hoof pawed at the ground, and the creature stepped towards the gate.

An old lady stood on the stage now, bearing witness to the boy's transgressions. "I saw him reach right into Hilda's apron and come out with a fistful of coins!"

Murmurs rippled over the crowd. A banana peel landed on the stage, not quite reaching its target. The boy jerked his head, and his hood fell back from his face. Sweat glistened from his forehead.

Fable frowned and threw her thoughts back onto the gate. "C'mon," she said under breath. She panted as the lever inched upward.

The goat stretched her neck up and sniffed at the lever. With a nudge from her nose, it popped open.

The doe reared up on her hind legs and landed with a gleeful bleat. Fable cheered inwardly. She willed the animal to give the gate a push.

On the stage, Murphy crossed his arms and shook his head as he listened to the lady go on and on with ever-more-unlikely tales of the boy's transgressions. "All right, all right." He waved the lady off the stage. "I'm sure there are many more witnesses to these heinous crimes, but I think we have enough to sentence the boy."

One of the guards helped the woman down the stairs. The man with the ax spun it around over his head, and the audience laughed and cheered.

Fable's chest tightened. She had to do something to make this work, fast. She concentrated on the gate, and it inched open a crack. *Come on, goat! I need a little help!*

The nanny goat butted the gate with her head, and it swung all the way open. She stood for a moment, her eyes wide, as she drank in the freedom in front of her. With a bleat, she reared up and burst out of the pen, then ran straight into the trees.

The other animals didn't notice. The hogs snoozed in their straw bed. The grey horse near the back yawned and shook his head.

Darn! Fable looked at Thorn, who still stood near the stage trying to watch Fable out of the corner of her eye.

Thorn's nose wrinkled, a look of confusion on her face. She waved at Fable and mouthed, "What are we doing?"

Fable held up her finger. "Wait," she mouthed back.

Murphy was belting out a compelling speech on the merits of the law and the evils of thievery. The crowd hung on Murphy's every word as the guards untied the boy's hands and laid his left arm across the table.

Fable's panic rose from her chest, skipped over her

throat, and landed squarely in her head. She whirled towards the animal pen, and a burst of energy leapt from her. The air rippled and the waves hit the back fence with a deafening *crack*.

The startled animals bolted around the pen, wild-eyed and squealing, clucking or braying with fear.

Fable froze. Murphy broke off speaking. The entire crowd turned to see where the sound had come from.

Murphy squinted, his hand over his eyes, and peered back towards the pen. "Who left the gate open?" he shouted. "Somebody close it. Immediately!"

One of his kitchen boys ran back to the corral. Fable aimed her hands towards him, intending to raise a small root to trip him. Instead, a surge of power shot from her hands and the ground erupted under his feet. Wind howled through the clearing. It knocked the kitchen boy over and blinded the crowd with dirt and debris.

Chaos erupted. The animals, in a mix of terror and the realization that they were free, bolted in every direction. Three hogs ran onto the stage, squealing, and knocked over the table and guards in a swarm of flying hooves and pink hide. Cows and horses barreled through the crowd. Murphy lifted his robes and ran towards the back door of the Buttertub. Fable rushed through the mob of panicked patrons and animals towards the stage.

"Now, Thorn. Grab him!"

Thorn, her eyes wide with shock, tore her gaze away from Fable and leapt up the stairs in two strides. The boy hid behind the table and scrambled away from her. Thorn grunted and grabbed onto his leg. She dragged him towards her by the ankle and slung him like a rag doll over her shoulder.

A woman pointed at her. "Hey, that beast is stealing the thief!"

Thorn's feet battered the boards as she ran down the stairs and through the crowd. Fable tried to run, but somebody snatched her bag and pulled her back. She twisted around. The drunken man from the corral stood behind her, one meaty fist latched onto her precious bag. She scowled.

"This one did something. I saw her. She magic'd!" He grabbed her arms and pinned them to her side. Fable glared at him. His pockmarked face sneered down at her with a toothless grin.

"Fable! Duck!" Thorn cried out, and Fable did just that.

The frying pan swung over her head and hit the man squarely in the face. His hands went limp around

Fable's arms. He spun in a perfect circle and hit the ground, knocked out cold.

Thorn thrust the pan into Fable's hand, grabbed her around the waist and took off as fast as she could for the forest, a human over each shoulder.

Footsteps pounded behind them. The two guards from the stage charged after the trio, quickly gaining ground.

Thorn seemed to be struggling under the added weight of the two young humans. With an uneven stride, she reached the spot where she had left her ax and paused. She fumbled with it, trying to balance the boy over her shoulder and pick it up at the same time.

Star stepped onto the path behind them. With her chest puffed and feathers ruffled, she turned to face the charging guards. Her beak opened wide and released a thunderous rush of heat and fire. Everything within ten feet of the Firehawk's mouth burst into flames.

A wave of heat passed over Fable and the others. The guards stopped in their tracks in front of the flames, mouths gaped open. They turned tail and ran back for the Buttertub, stumbling and tripping in their hurry to get away from the fire-breathing bird.

Thorn panted as she lowered Fable onto the ground. She threw the thief down beside her.

"You owe us." She glowered down at him.

He coughed from the smoke and looked back and forth between Fable and her giant grey friend with the fiery yellow eyes. Finally, his gaze rested on the mottled-brown chicken. She still stood behind them, gazing with pride at the fire she'd created. It was beginning to burn itself out, leaving blackened char behind.

Star walked to Fable's feet and tugged on the bottom of her dress with her beak. "My dear, we are at the Lichwood. This is where we must part ways."

She peeked around Fable at the path that lay ahead of them and shuffled her feet. Fable squatted down, and the hen nuzzled up into her arms.

"I'll miss you. Thank you for your help. Are you sure you'll be able to find your flock?"

"I can sense their auras now. They're waiting for me at the edge of the Burntwood." Star nibbled on a dark lock of Fable's hair. "I know we'll meet again. Good luck, dear."

"Bye." Fable sniffled.

With a wave of her tail feathers, Star turned and strutted back towards the Buttertub. Fable watched until she disappeared around the bend.

Thorn cleared her throat. "We need to go." She

prodded the boy with the end of her ax. "You can follow us out of here or stay behind to deal with Murphy. Your choice."

He looked at her warily and got to his feet. Then he glanced back over his shoulder at the scorched ground and the Buttertub in the distance.

The guards had gathered in front of the tavern. Murphy's frantic voice filled the air. "Find that boy!"

The thief grimaced. "Lead the way." He tugged his hood back over his wavy black hair, his face swollen and tired.

The Lichwood

Despite the forest being green and full, Fable felt uneasy. The Burntwood, while looking desolate, had felt safe and had held the spark of new beginnings. The sun had shone brightly through the blackened branches, offering warmth and hope. In comparison, the Lichwood felt dark and foreboding. It was eerily quiet. There were no sounds of chattering squirrels, buzzing bees, or any sign of normal forest life at all. Just the silent trees and the fungi growing around their roots.

Thorn, her presence steady and comforting, led the way. The boy walked behind her, gazing up into the trees above his head, and Fable brought up the rear. The air pressed down around them, heavy and dense.

After a few minutes of walking, Thorn stopped and faced Fable and the boy.

"Give me a minute." Thorn dropped her backpack to the ground behind her. Her face was red, her eyes burning yellow.

101

Fable nodded. "Go ahead. We'll wait here."

The lumbering girl pushed her way through the trees, crunching and crashing as she went, and disappeared.

The boy watched her leave with an anxious expression. "Where's she going?"

"To meditate."

Fable's shoulder ached from the weight of her bag. She shrugged it off and patted the side, feeling for the hard leather cover beneath the fabric. Her cargo was behaving exactly like a normal book.

The boy raised a brow. "Meditate?"

"It calms her down." Fable sat down beside her bag on the dirt path. "Trust me, it's better for all of us when she's calm."

The boy looked thoughtful, examining the trampled trail of broken branches Thorn had left through the trees.

"Yeah." He sat down next to her. "You know, I could take off right now and you couldn't stop me."

Fable shrugged. "You could. But where would you go? Back to the tavern where they'll cut off your hand?"

The boy's face turned red and his gaze darted away from her.

"That was really rotten, what you did in the

102

Buttertub," Fable said. "Tricking me like that."

The boy reached down, pulled a blade of grass from the dirt, and examined it. "Sorry. I didn't mean to upset you. I was hungry. I don't have any money."

"Why didn't you just go home, then?" Fable asked.

"I don't have a home."

"Oh."

"My family went missing a few weeks ago." He bit his bottom lip. "I don't have anything."

"What happened?"

The boy sighed. "We were on the road. We're travelling entertainers, and we live in a motorhome. We were visiting Mistford for a festival, but my parents never made it to the stage. I don't know what happened."

A lump rose in Fable's throat. "I'm sorry."

They were silent for a few minutes. The boy twisted and twirled the blade of grass through his fingers.

"I'm Fable. What's your name?"

"Brennus." He stood up and bowed with a flourish. "Of the Trilling Tanagers. Or I was anyway. Before they disappeared."

Fable sat on her haunches and regarded him with interest. "You can sing?"

"I'm better at the guitar. But I left it behind in the camper. It's too heavy to carry around on foot."

Crashing sounds came from the trees to their left and Thorn emerged. She was back to her usual self. Intimidating, large, and her skin was its normal shade of bluish-grey.

Fable met her friend's olive-green eyes. "Feeling better?"

Thorn nodded and sat next to her friend on the mossy earth. She glared at Brennus. "Do you know what this girl's done for you?"

"I . . . well, yes. I do." Colour crept over his cheeks. "I said I was sorry. I didn't mean to hurt her feelings."

Thorn put her arm around Fable. Fable smiled. It felt good to have a friend by her side. She'd never had a close friend before, other than Timothy. And as her cousin and roommate, he didn't have much choice. She cleared her throat.

"This is Brennus. He lost his family, too. Do you think the Fey Witch can help him?"

"If anybody can help him, it's the Fey Witch."

Fable turned to Brennus. "Do you want to come with us? I'm looking for my cousin, and Thorn's family is missing too. We're going to the Fey Witch for help."

Brennus shoved his hands into his pockets and shrugged, kicking the ground with a dirty sneaker. "I don't have anywhere else to go."

"Let's get a move on, then." Thorn heaved herself

back to her feet.

Fable followed her friend's lead. She brushed the dirt off her dress and slid her bag onto her shoulder.

The woods grew thicker and darker the further they walked. Fable missed the bright, sunny Burntwood Forest. A feeling of dread crept over her. Thorn checked behind her back every so often, and Brennus jumped at every twig that snapped under their feet.

"Are you sure this is the right way?" Brennus asked Thorn.

"Do you see any other way?" she snapped back.

Fable looked at the trees surrounding them. The path ran in one direction. They hadn't seen any forks or turns.

"Don't you have a map?" Brennus batted away a low-hanging branch.

"Folkvars don't need maps." Thorn tapped the side of her head with her pointer finger. "We're woodspeople. We have an innate sense of direction."

Brennus shook his head and turned to Fable. "What about you? Can't you use your magic to just zap us to the Fey Witch?" He snapped his fingers.

Fable swallowed. *As if. I'd probably transport us into that dragon's den Thorn talked about.* "I don't think it works like that. Besides, I trust Thorn." Fable hoped he would drop the topic of her magic.

"Oh." Brennus hunched his shoulders and kicked a rock down the path ahead of him. It bounced off the back of Thorn's calf.

She stopped and glanced back over her shoulder with a scowl. "You're welcome to leave us and head out on your own."

Brennus glanced into the trees and frowned. "I'll stick with you. No map, no magic. You'll need my help."

Thorn snorted. "Right."

"Come on, you guys." Fable wanted to put as much space between them and the Buttertub as possible before nightfall. She was sure Murphy would send more guards after them.

They continued down the path, but the silence only lasted a few minutes.

Brennus spoke up. "You know, I've heard this forest is called Lichwood because it's controlled by a Lich."

"Not possible." Thorn thumped the handle of her ax on the ground in time with her feet. "There hasn't been a Lich in Starfell for years. Not since Endora, and she was killed ages ago."

Endora. That name those men mentioned in the tavern.

"You can't destroy a Lich." Brennus grabbed at

a bush and snapped off a twig. "You can destroy her powers, but she'll build them back up. It wouldn't surprise me if Endora controlled this place again." He shuddered. "There's a reason nobody comes in here."

"What's a Lich?" Fable had never heard the word before. In Larkmoor, nobody spoke of evil or foul things. Such things simply didn't exist.

"A Lich is somebody who was once a powerful witch, or a wizard, or maybe a sorcerer. One who's gone bad." Brennus lowered his voice. "They spend years practicing dark magic and learn how to become immortal. It's done through evil acts, like killing. And they need to keep sacrificing souls to stay alive."

Fable shivered. "That sounds horrible."

"They're very rare," Thorn said. "And this wood's been quiet for years."

The longer they walked, the darker it became. Fable wasn't sure if it was because the trees were getting thicker or if night was starting to fall.

Thorn stopped abruptly in the middle of the trail.

Brennus walked face-first into her backpack. "Oomph!"

Thorn studied the trees, turning to face them. "Let's make camp."

"Is it safe?" Fable couldn't shake the prickly sensation that crawled up her spine.

"I don't think anything lives in here." Thorn squinted into the dark branches around them. "I don't want to keep hiking in the dark."

Brennus agreed. Thorn picked out a little spot between some trees just off the trail and unrolled the tent from her bag.

Fable peered into the forest, clutching her book bag tightly to her chest. The trees' gnarled branches seemed to reach out for them like skeletal hands. A tingling spread through her chest and she gulped for air. She hoped this was all worth it—that the Fey Witch could help, and they would find Timothy and her companions' families safe. And soon. She wondered what her cousin was doing this moment and if he was worried about her too.

Brennus looked at her with a wary expression. "You okay?"

"I'm fine." Fable cast him a sheepish look. With a final glance into the murky gloom of the branches above them, she turned and helped Thorn set up camp.

THIRTEEN

Friends and Magic

Cold seeped from the black trees right through the knit sweater and deep into Fable's bones.

"Should we start a fire?"

"I'd love to." Thorn grunted as she pounded a tent peg into the earth with the handle of her ax. "But there's nothing to burn."

Fable looked around at the forest floor. She noticed that there were no branches, twigs or sticks on the ground. It looked like somebody, or something, had picked the area clean.

"Can you use your magic?" Thorn thumped in another tent peg.

Fable sighed. She couldn't avoid the topic this time. Not after that day's events. Thorn and Brennus had seen what she could do. Fable's face grew hot. *And how I lose control.*

She shifted her feet. "Well, I—"

"Yeah." Brennus' eyes lit up. "You healed my hand. You blew up the livestock pen!"

"I'm not very good with it. Bad things happen when I use it."

"You saved me," Brennus said. "And it was awesome!"

"The explosion was my favourite part." Thorn chuckled. "Did you see that kitchen boy go flying?"

"Or Murphy's face when the pigs started chasing him."

Thorn grinned at Brennus. "Or *your* face when I grabbed you off that stage."

The three new friends burst into laughter. The heaviness in the air seemed to lift, and even the reaching branches didn't seem so scary anymore.

"I really didn't mean to do all that." Fable giggled. "But I guess it worked."

"Thank the gods." Brennus replied. He held out his wrist and flexed his fingers. "I still have two hands, thanks to you."

Thorn shrugged her shoulders, then bent to unpack the fly of the tent.

Fable smiled. "Okay. Let's do this. I need something to catch the flame. Some dried twigs or grass."

Brennus walked over to the nearest tree and pulled off some dried bark and moss. "Will this work?"

"Sure."

She gathered some rocks and crouched down to the

earth, using them to create a small circle. "I'll keep it small and contained. Just enough to warm up."

A branch snagged Fable's sweater when she stood. She jumped and let out a small yelp, her heart in her throat.

Brennus laughed. "Scared?"

"No." Fable grinned sheepishly. She eyed the forest around them, wondering what kind of creatures roamed there in the night. She shivered. *I'm not scared. But still, a protection spell wouldn't hurt.*

She rubbed her hands together and searched her mind for the song she had heard Aunt Moira sing that night when she had enchanted their yard.

The language had been both foreign and familiar to her. Fable opened her mouth and began singing, the words rolling effortlessly off her tongue. They came as naturally to her as breathing.

As she sang, she walked slowly around their camp in a large circle, her hand trailing behind her. A blue light shimmered from her fingertips and faded into the air.

When she finished, her heart was beating hard in her chest. *What was that?*

Brennus sat watching her in wide-eyed wonder. "Wow."

Thorn had stopped propping up the tent to listen.

"That's something I learned from my aunt, I guess." Fable reached out her hand and touched the air where the blue light had glistened moments before. The now-familiar rough, invisible wall met her fingers.

She let out a breath. "I think the song worked. There's a barrier. We should be safe from anything, or anybody, lurking around the forest tonight."

Thorn shook her head. "I've never seen anything like that. Amazing."

Fable flushed, smiling.

Brennus had filled the makeshift stone fire pit with bark and dried moss. He motioned Fable over, and she squatted beside it, holding out her hands. She rubbed them together slowly.

A small flicker of heat sparked between her palms. When she opened her eyes, a flame crackled from the ground, growing as more of the bark caught.

"You're something else, you know that?" Brennus looked at her in awe. He sat cross-legged in front of the small fire and warmed his hands over it.

Fable couldn't stop grinning.

Her job complete, Thorn came and sat next to them. She had the frying pan in her hand, which she set on the ground in front of her. There was a paper bag in her other hand. She reached inside, pulled out some apples and handed one to each of them.

"This should hold you over until supper's ready." She dumped some mushrooms into the pan and held it over the fire.

"This is so good. Thanks." Fable bit into the apple, its sweet juices running down her chin. After the rescue and a long afternoon hiking through the woods, she felt like she could devour a whole bushel of apples. Nearly as soon as she had begun, she was licking the juice off of her fingers.

Brennus licked his lips with a satisfied smile. "Where did you get all this food?"

Thorn shrugged as she stirred the mushrooms. "Folkvars live off the land. We garden and forage for food. Ever since I was a toddler I've gone with my parents into the woods. Mushrooms, nuts, berries . . . my mom would make the best bramble-berry jam." She looked wistfully into the darkness beyond the fire.

"We'll find them, Thorn," Fable said gently.

Thorn gave her a small smile and stirred the food again.

When supper was ready, Thorn passed them both rough wooden spoons, and after a few minutes, the three of them sat around the pan and shared the small meal.

Satisfied, Fable untied the book bag at her feet and slid out the *Book of Chaos*, placing it on her lap.

Despite knowing that it held no clues, she couldn't help but hope that something had changed.

She opened the cover and flipped through the pages. They glared in the firelight, blank. There were no words or secret codes or clues. It looked exactly the same as it had the day before.

She sighed and closed it with a snap.

"Your book," Brennus said, his mouth full. "I know that pattern."

Fable looked down at the twisting vines. "You do?"

"It's the pattern on my dad's guitar." Brennus took it from Fable's lap. He held it up to his face, studying the pattern.

Fable fought the urge to snatch it back. Maybe he would know more about it.

He ran his fingers over the painting and paused on one of the skulls. It had a wide, evil smile and a rotting vine winding through its mouth.

"Creepy, isn't it?" he whispered.

"Yeah."

Brennus handed the book back to her, his eyes glistening. He wiped away the moisture and sniffed.

"My dad only had that guitar for a few days. We were on our way to Mistford for the music festival when we saw an old lady on the side of the road with boxes of odds and ends for sale. She was really old, with these weird purple eyes. Kind of like yours." The firelight flickered across his face.

"My dad is always looking for a bargain, so he stopped to barter. Once she heard that we were entertainers, she pulled out an old guitar. She told Dad it was magic, and when he played it, the song would entrance the crowd. She said that he would never want for money again."

Thorn grunted.

"She looked like an old hedge witch, the kind that tells fortunes at county fairs. Dad believed her. He bought the guitar and we went on our way. That night we stopped and played at a tavern. We made three times as much money as we normally would."

"So it worked." Fable could see the man, singing and playing. Like the audience of the guitar's song, she was entranced by the story.

"It sure did. That night, anyways. He was so excited, he couldn't wait to use it on the bigger crowds in Mistford."

He paused, his hands clenched on his knees. "When we got there, I went to play my guitar for a group of kids. My parents went to the ale yards, but they never made it onto the stage. When I went to find them, nobody'd seen them and they'd missed their turn to play. I looked behind the stage, where they would've waited. They weren't there. Not even the guitar."

He swallowed and stared off over the fire into the darkness. "It was really weird. There was black soot all over the ground, like there had been a fire. I never did find my parents. Nobody I talked to had heard from them."

"That's awful," Fable whispered.

"The folks who run the festival told me that they probably just ran off. Left me behind." Brennus choked out a laugh. "Nobody would help me."

Thorn cleared her throat. "The same thing happened to my sister. She bought her bow off an old lady selling trinkets on the road. She said it would never miss its target. The fire was that night. I lost her and my parents in the chaos when we ran. I haven't seen them since."

They sat in silence for a moment. Thorn eyed the book on Fable's lap. "Is that book why you're here?"

Fable nodded her head. She hadn't planned to tell anybody about it, ashamed that she had triggered the book and lost Timothy. But Thorn and Brennus made her feel safe. The book must be linked to their stories somehow—there were too many similarities between them to be a coincidence. She was determined to find Timothy, and maybe they could help each other.

"Yes." She stared into the fire. "I found it in my bookcase, back in Larkmoor."

She told them the whole story. About the nightmare, the tendrils that had escaped from the book, and how she and Timothy had tried to destroy it. How it had pulled Timothy into its pages, and she'd followed and ended up in the Burntwood Forest. She told them about her magic, about how in Larkmoor it was something to hide. About how ashamed she was, and how she thought it was her fault that the book went off and took Timothy from Rose Cottage.

After her story, she wiped tears from her eyes. Thorn reached over and pulled her sideways off her seat into a hug. Fable sniffed, and a smile broke through her tears.

"Thanks, Thorn."

"It's not your fault." Thorn released her and patted her back. "I think there's something bad going on in Starfell."

"It does seem pretty crazy how our stories are tied together," Brennus said.

"I hope the Fey Witch has some answers."

It was completely dark now, and they were all tired. Fable returned the book to her bag and put out the fire. Thorn packed up what was left of the food. She crawled into the tent first, and then Brennus joined her. Fable carried the book bag to the tent and placed it in the corner by the door. As she snuggled down into

117

the sleeping bag next to Thorn, the Folkvar girl cleared her throat.

Fable lifted her head and peered toward the black heap that was her friend's figure. "Thorn? What's wrong?"

"I just want to say . . ." Thorn paused. "I think you're a really good magician. Or witch. Or sorceress. Whatever you are."

Fable smiled. "Thank you."

Unwelcome Companions

The next day, they continued further into the depths of the Lichwood Forest. As they walked, Thorn regaled them with stories she had heard about how the Fey Witch had helped farmers' crops grow in years of drought, found lost children, and healed life-threatening illness.

"The next day, little Birch was walking again." Thorn nodded as she finished telling them about a Folkvar boy who had broken both of his legs falling from a tree. According to her, Birch's mother had sent a letter to the Fey Witch for help.

"That's amazing," Fable said, feeling hopeful. If these stories were true, the Fey Witch would certainly be able to help them. Wouldn't she?

"Who told you this story?" Brennus asked. "Did you see Birch walking the next day?"

"My mother told me," Thorn gave him a side-ways glance. "It happened before I was born."

"Where was this Fey Witch when the Greenwood

went up in flames? These all sound like tall tales to me," Brennus scrunched up his nose and ducked under a branch. "Do you even know what her house looks like?"

Thorn grunted and said they would know when they reached their destination. "The Fey Witch is very private, very mysterious. We'll know we're there when we get there."

By afternoon, the trees had thinned noticeably. Sunspots danced through the branches and dappled the forest floor. Fable breathed in the clean smell of loamy earth and green leaves. She found herself enjoying the walk.

"What's Larkmoor like?" Brennus asked from in front of Fable.

Boring.

"It's very . . . ordinary," she replied, wondering if he'd even know what that meant to her. "It's a small town without much excitement. Nobody else has magic."

Nobody gets their hands cut off for stealing, either.

"But it's safe."

"Nobody there has magic?" Brennus asked with a note of disbelief. He walked in front of Fable, struggling to keep up with the Folkvar's long strides in front of him. "But then, how do you?"

Fable shrugged. "I wasn't born there."

"Where were you born?"

"Mistford," Fable replied. "My aunt moved us to Larkmoor when her husband and my parents died in a rock slide." She paused, her tongue stuck in her throat. She tried not to think about her parents, or what life would have been like in Mistford.

"Aunt Moira got a job there, so that's where we went. I was only three, and she was pregnant with Timothy. I don't really remember Mistford. My first memories are of baby Timothy. I used to make pink bubbles for him—they would float from my finger tips. He would laugh and try to pop them. I didn't know it was magic until my aunt caught me. She started to yell at me for it but ended up in a fit of giggles."

A wave of homesickness washed over her. She missed her aunt, and Timothy, and Grimm. Even their safe, simple life in Rose Cottage. What she wouldn't give to be curled up with a book and a cup of tea. Grimm would be beside her and Timothy would be playing his video game on the floor, with Aunt Moira puttering around in the kitchen making more tea. She dropped her gaze to the ground as they walked.

A loud crowing broke the silence. Fable and her friends stopped, looking up into the trees. With a flutter of dark wings and more frantic cawing, several crows burst from the trees in front of them into the sky above. The foreboding sound of their cries echoed in the unnatural silence of the forest.

"That's the first sign of life I've seen here," Fable said.

Thorn put her hand in air to silence them. She cocked her head, listening.

Fable held her breath. A quiet rustling came from the underbrush to her left. She couldn't see any movement, but there was a soft padding noise that reminded her of Grimm's footsteps in the forest behind Rose Cottage.

Thorn's unruly hair whipped around her shoulders as she looked from side to side with a fierce stare. She fixed her blazing yellow eyes on her companions.

"Run!"

Fable and Brennus looked at each other, both frozen with fear. Thorn pushed Fable forward, and she stumbled and almost fell.

"Go!"

Out of the corner of her eye, Fable saw a mass of black fur and gleaming white teeth leap out of the trees behind Thorn. Snarling, the beast tried to lock its jaws around Thorn's leg. Thorn kicked at it, and it yelped. A glint of sunlight flashed off Thorn's ax as she swung it through the air.

Without another backwards glance, Fable ran. Her

feet pounded against the ground, and her book bag thumped on her side. She heard Brennus' footsteps behind her. Focused on the trail, she barely registered the dark form in the trees beside her.

"Fable!" Brennus shouted. He grabbed her bag and pulled her to a sudden stop.

A black wolf-like creature, who was at least twice the size of Grimm, leapt from trees onto the trail in front of her. Its hair stood on end, and its lips were pulled back in a menacing grimace full of razor-sharp teeth, with a rasping growl to match. It blocked their path, glowing red eyes locked on Fable. The hot breath that filled the space between them smelled of rotting meat and made Fable gag.

She held her breath. *Nice dog, good boy.* She tried to send calming energy toward the beast. It snapped at the air with its vise-like jowls.

Magic. Use your magic!

She kept eye contact with the sinister creature and concentrated on building the familiar warm energy within herself. Her hands shook as she rubbed them together with barely noticeable movements.

The beast lunged. Fable threw her arms up in front of her face. Brennus grabbed her around the waist and pulled her back, out of the giant wolf's reach. Snapping at her again, it caught the hem of her dress and pulled.

123

Brennus lost his grip and Fable fell to the ground. The creature dragged her back towards the trees.

She screamed and kicked, grass and gravel burning her thighs as she was dragged, but it only picked up speed. Rocks and roots tore at her clothes as she slid sideways over the forest floor. Through the chaos of the world spinning around her, she caught sight of Brennus sprinting through the underbrush.

She tensed, anger igniting a burning fire in the pit of her stomach. She reached out and took hold of a low-hanging branch. It tore from the tree with enough force to slow the hound for just a moment—long enough for Fable to swing wildly with the branch, smashing it into the creature's face. High-pitched yelps filled the air.

It let go of Fable's dress, biting at the stick in her hand. She scrambled backwards and stood to face the beast.

It snarled through curled lips, crouching back onto its haunches, hackles raised. Then it launched itself into the air towards her.

Fable stood her ground and shouted "No!" with all her might.

Magical energy exploded from her. Trees bent backwards. Leaves and sticks flew through the air.

The air around the creature rippled, and it stumbled and landed in the dirt.

All became still. The only noises were Fable's gasping breaths.

The beast raised its head. Casting a fearful look at Fable, it scrambled to its feet and ran off into the woods, yips and whines trailing through the air.

"Fable?" came Thorn's voice from behind her.

Fable spun around to face her friends. Brennus' mouth hung open.

"I'm okay."

Thorn nodded. "Let's go. Fast, before they tell their friends. They'll be back."

Fable smoothed out her tattered dress and eyed the scrapes and gravel burns on her arms and legs. Satisfied that none of the wounds were in immediate need of attention, she adjusted the bag around her shoulder. When her hand grazed it, the fabric felt warm. Was it from the book? Or the heat of her body? She didn't have time to look.

Brennus took the lead, Fable came next, with Thorn following behind, urging them to go faster. A chorus of howls erupted behind them. With a burst of adrenaline, Fable broke into a run.

Branches whipped in Fable's face and caught at the remains of her dress. Ahead of her, Brennus stumbled and caught himself, lurching forward into a sprint again. Thorn crashed along behind. The howling grew closer.

Fable's legs ached. She stumbled over a root across the trail and barely righted herself. She couldn't keep up this pace much longer.

They couldn't outrun the hounds, and Fable didn't think she could muster the energy to fight off another one with magic. But the bays and barks still gained on them.

She glanced back at Thorn, who looked as tired as she felt. Brennus' pace lagged. There was only one option left—they would have to hide.

They rounded a bend in the trail and passed a large spruce tree with a trunk as wide as Thorn was tall. Bright sunlight hit Fable's face. Their pounding feet landed on soft green grass that rippled out through the meadow that opened in front of them.

A small circular stone house stood in the centre of the clearing. Vines covered with dainty pink flowers grew over the thatched roof and down the side. A sky-blue door caught Fable's eye through the flora.

"The cottage!" She dashed forward, and her friends followed.

Something crashed behind them. She looked over her shoulder and choked at the sight of a snarling canine face through the trees. Thorn grabbed the back of Fable's dress bodice, lifting her feet from the ground, then tucked Fable under her arm. Brennus already bounced along over the Folkvar's other shoulder.

Thorn sprinted toward the house. With barely a pause, she leaned back and kicked the door. The latch cracked as it burst open. Thorn stepped inside, dropped the two humans on the wooden floor, and slammed the door behind her. She threw the bar over the door and then leaned on it, panting for breath.

Fable rolled across the floor, her bag and its heavy contents swinging wildly until she tumbled into a pile of books. Her bag hit her squarely in the head. She sat up, bewildered, in a dimly-lit room that was overflowing with piles of books and plants, with dried herbs hanging from the ceiling.

"Oh!" came a surprised voice from behind them.

Brennus struggled to sit up, and Thorn and Fable whirled to face the frail old man who had spoken.

"Well, hello there," he said, smiling. "Welcome to Tulip Manor."

Fedilmid Coot

The old man sat at a long oak table at the far end of the room that was piled high with books, papers and a potted geranium. Before him lay an open book and a handmade blue-and-white ceramic mug. He had a sleekly groomed grey beard and kind, sparkling blue eyes. His long dark-blue robe brushed the floor, and his fingers were adorned with jewelled rings. Small round spectacles sat perched on the tip of his nose. Fable liked him immediately.

The hounds had caught up to them. They threw themselves at the door with manic bays and howls, shaking it every time they slammed against it. Thorn ignored them, her eyes closed, quietly muttering to herself.

Brennus stood up and reached out a hand towards Fable. She let him help her to her feet.

"Pay them no mind," the man said. He stood from the table and clasped his hands in front of him. "They won't get in here. I've enchanted the place against any who would do me harm." He glanced at the door as one of the hounds let out an angry howl from behind it. He walked to the door and, pushing Thorn aside, removed the bar and opened it.

Brennus let out an involuntary yelp.

"Sir!" Fable's heart leapt into her throat.

The hounds outside slammed against an invisible barrier in the doorway, growling and baring their teeth.

"Just as I thought." The old man clucked his tongue. "Their intentions are definitely not good. If they were friendly, they would have waltzed right in here." He closed the door on their snarling faces and turned to the children. "Sit down a spell, I'll make more tea."

Fable shuffled her feet. *Who is this guy?* His magic reminded her of Aunt Moira's.

The man unhooked the old iron kettle from a hook inside the stone fireplace and refilled it from a decanter of water on the mantle, then rehung it above the crackling fire. Whistling a happy tune, he stepped into the kitchen area, grabbed three mugs from the cupboard, and lined them up on the counter.

The baying hounds lunged at the kitchen window above the sink, snarling, with drool flying from their lips. The man simply closed the curtains and ignored them.

Fable and her friends stood frozen by the door,

gaping at him.

He turned and stopped short. "Sit down, sit down." He motioned towards the living area.

"Thank you," Fable said.

She and Brennus picked their way through piles of books and potted plants to sit on a small couch, covered with a colourful patched quilt, which faced the stone hearth. Brennus moved several magazines and a cactus in a terracotta pot before he could sit. Tall bookshelves lined the curved walls.

Thorn stayed by the door, counting under her breath.

Once settled, Fable took in the tiny cottage. It had a large, circular room for all the living areas, and a straight wall in the back with a door that must lead to a bedroom. The only light came from patches of sunlight streaming through windows placed haphazardly around the outside, making the space feel cozy and inviting. There were books and plants in every nook and cranny. Despite the clutter, it was a lovely home. One of those places that make you feel welcome as soon as you come through the door.

Her gaze rested on the wizened old man, who was plucking leaves from a bundle of dried herbs which hung above the counter and then dropping them into the mugs. His navy-blue robe swished around him, and the silver star patches at the hem caught her eye. She glanced down at her book bag. It matched his robes perfectly. What an odd coincidence.

"Sir, your robes . . ."

Her words were lost in another round of crashing and thumping from outside the house.

The old man glanced at the walls, then picked up a pot holder from the mantle and grabbed the whistling kettle from the fire. He carried it to the kitchen area and poured the water into the mugs. "Why are those nasty hounds after you?"

"We don't know," Fable replied.

Thorn, finished with her counting, squeezed herself into the armchair across from Fable and Brennus. She filled up the whole chair, her knees bent up past her elbows.

The old man walked into the seating area and handed each of them a steaming mug. Fable wrapped her hands around it, the warmth seeping through her fingers. She breathed in the familiar, soothing smell of peppermint.

"So, who might you be, then?" the man asked cheerfully. He scooped up his mug from the table and sat in the armchair across from Thorn.

Fable transferred the hot mug between her hands. "I'm Fable. This is Brennus and Thorn."

131

"And you are?" Brennus asked their host.

"My name is Fedilmid," the old man said. "Fedilmid Coot. What brings three young persons like yourselves to the Lichwood? Where are your parents?"

"We don't know. That's why we're here," Brennus said.

"Fable's are dead," Thorn added.

"Thorn!" Brennus glared at her.

"Well, they are." Thorn blushed. Her hand shook as she went to set her mug down on the table next to her chair. It tottered and sloshed tea over its edges.

"It's okay," Fable said. She turned to Fedilmid. "She's right, but they died a long time ago. I don't really remember them. I live with my aunt and cousin. These two are missing their parents." She nodded towards Brennus and Thorn. "But I've lost my cousin. And, well, I guess I'm kind of missing, too. From my home in Larkmoor."

Fedilmid took a sip from his mug. "Larkmoor, you say?"

"Yeah. I need to find my cousin and a way home. We're looking for the Fey Witch. Do you know her? Or how to find her?"

"The Fey Witch?" Fedilmid stood from his seat. "You're in luck! You've found him." He bowed with an extravagant flourish of his hand.

Thorn coughed and picked up her mug again to hide her face.

"You?" Brennus asked. "But I thought the Fey Witch was a—"

"Woman?" Fedilmid stood up straight, a hand on his hip. "Men can be witches too. There's no gender requirement for the job."

It was Brennus' turn to flush. "Oh, right. I didn't mean—"

"Oh, he meant nothing by it," Fable said. She grinned. She liked the man even more. He had an unpretentious air about him, and Fable recognized the magical current of energy flowing through his house. "Can you help us?"

"I can certainly try." Fedilmid rubbed his hands together with a gleam in his bright blue eyes. "I'm due for a little mystery and adventure. What clues have you got?"

Fable gingerly slid the book bag off her shoulder and placed it in her lap. "Just this."

Fedilmid stared at the bag, his eyes wide with wonder. "That material. Where did you get it?"

"From my aunt, Moira." Fable replied. "She gave it to me when I was little. Just a toddler."

He looked at her, his bushy brows furrowed, and then back at the bag. With a quick movement, he pulled open his robes to reveal pink fleece pajamas underneath. There was a pattern of yellow rubber ducks splashed across them.

Fable exchanged glances with her friends. Thorn shrugged her shoulders.

"Umm . . . nice ducks?" Brennus said.

"No, no." Fedilmid shook the right corner of his robe. "Right here! The hem!"

Fable eyed the star patches that matched her bag. "Yes, sir, I noticed—"

"You must be the Nuthatch girl!" Fedilmid jumped up and down.

"You knew my parents?"

"Does a cyclops eat blue cheese for breakfast?"

Fable and Brennus exchanged glances, and Brennus shrugged his shoulders.

"Yes! Of course he does." Fedilmid did a happy little jig in front of the hearth.

Fable's smile grew wider. Hope ignited within her at the thought of learning more about her family.

"Your mother needed a bag for the herbs she collected. I'd made this robe and had the extra material on hand. One night while she was sleeping, I whipped that bag up. I'll never forget her face when I handed it to her at breakfast the next morning. Such a dear woman."

Fable gazed down at the bag in her lap, running her hand over the soft blue wool. There was a catch in the back of her throat. *This was my mother's.* She hugged it to her chest.

"How did you know my mother?"

Fedilmid was about to answer when the door to the cottage swung open and the snarling barks of the hounds pierced the air.

Fable jumped off the couch, but no black snouts or gnashing teeth crashed into the room. Instead, in walked another old man with rich brown skin, a grey-streaked black beard, and broad shoulders. He carried a bulky canvas sack and wore a grey woolen tunic over his brown trousers. He slammed the door behind him.

"Fedilmid! What are those blasted dogs doing out there?"

SIXTEEN

The Nuthatches

The grizzled man gazed at them and paused, taking in the scene in front of him. "Oh. I see we have visitors." He dropped his heavy sack on the floor and smoothed out his frizzled beard. "Ah . . . hello."

"Hello," Brennus and Fable both said at once. Thorn eyed him from behind her mug.

"Children, this is my husband, Algar." Fedilmid tied his robe shut around his waist. "Algar, this is Fable, Brennus, and Thorn. They've come to seek help from the Fey Witch."

"Ah." Algar nodded. He picked up the sack, shuffled into the kitchen and heaved it onto the counter. "I better get supper going, then. You came on the right day—you won't believe what I found."

He opened the sack and took three rabbits out, hides removed, and laid them on the counter. Thorn turned away, a look of horror on her face.

"Rabbits!" Fedilmid exclaimed. He clapped his

hands. "How far did you have to go to find those?"

"Almost halfway back to the Buttertub." Algar smiled, laugh lines crinkling around his eyes. He rummaged through the drawer beneath the sink and pulled out a large butcher knife, then began to slice the meat.

"I'm sure you've noticed—the woods are very quiet now." Fedilmid clicked his tongue. "When Jinny Greentoes went missing, all the animals cleared out. Something spooked them."

"Jinny Greentoes?" Fable asked.

As Algar prepared dinner, Fedilmid told his tale.

"Jinny Greentoes was another witch who resided in the Lichwood Forest years ago. She lived in a cabin beside the river, not far from here. We were neighbours, good friends. She was very old. Older than I by a stretch. At one time, she was a powerful witch, but her magic had faded with age."

Fedilmid sat down in his chair. "Algar and I often visited her and helped her around her home. We shoveled snow, cleaned her gutters, all the odds and ends she couldn't manage with her own magic anymore. In exchange, she baked us cookies, bread, and all sorts of treats. My waistline suffered a lot in those years." He patted his belly with a grin.

Taking a sip of his tea, he continued. "About

twelve years ago, she vanished without a trace. I thought perhaps she'd finally gone to live with one of her children. Her sons had tried for years to get her to move into Mistford so they could look after her."

"Mistford? That's where my parents were from," Fable said.

Brennus nodded. "And where mine went missing."

"It's a popular place. Beautiful in the fall when the leaves are all changing." Algar rubbed spices onto the meat on the counter in front of him.

Fedilmid chuckled, lost in thought. "Jinny was fiercely independent, always fighting the idea of leaving her home. But she was struggling on her own. When she disappeared, we thought her sons had finally won her over. Not giving it another thought, Algar and I continued on without any worries, other than for our lost crumpets and cakes."

Algar nodded from the kitchen. He placed sliced meat into the cast iron pan on the stove. It sizzled and spit when he prodded it.

"It was several years before we heard anything of her again."

"Did she know my parents, too?" Fable asked.

"Patience, child." Fedilmid winked at her. "I met your parents when they arrived at my door one night, a couple years later. Now that I think of it, they made an entrance much like you three." He smiled. "Although they were being chased by Undead. A bit scarier than hounds, if you ask me."

Brennus gulped, gripped by Fedilmid and the tale. "Undead?"

"Recently risen," Algar said. "We weren't sure where they came from, probably some wayward sorcerer trying to cause havoc. They didn't last long, we found them back to being dead near the front step the next morning."

Thorn shuddered and uncrossed her legs. "That sounds horrible."

"Yes, and we had to re-bury them a long way from here. It took us a whole day. Didn't want them to come back and find us again." Algar flipped the meat in the pan a little too aggressively, causing oil to splatter on the stove.

"It was awful, but my enchantment on the house held, and we were all okay. Fable, your parents had your uncle, Thomas, with them." Fedilmid chuckled as he reminisced. "Quite the adventurous group, Faari, Morton, and Thomas."

Fable sat on the edge of her chair, leaning towards him. "Aunt Moira said they used to go on all kinds of adventures."

"They were searching for Jinny Greentoes when

they arrived here." Fedilmid nodded. "She had information they required regarding a quest they were on." He shook his head. "I told them that the cabin was empty. They stayed here for a few weeks while they searched, but they came up with nothing. We had so much fun, though. They were charming guests, so grateful and kind."

He paused and looked at Fable. His voice softened. "They ran into trouble after they left here."

Fable sat back in her chair and looked at her hands. "Aunt Moira said they died in a rock slide on their way home from a journey to the mountains."

Thorn, leaning forward with her elbows on her knees in rapt attention, gave Fable an empathetic look.

Fedilmid raised his eye brows. "Did she, now? Did she tell you anything else about the, ah . . . unfortunate situation?"

Fable shook her head. "No. She won't talk much about them anymore. She moved us to Rose Cottage in Larkmoor because she got a job there. We have no other family. Timothy, my cousin—Thomas' son—is missing. He got sucked into the Burntwood Forest by magic, and when I came after him, he was gone." She took a deep breath to steady her nerves. "I have to find him. And Thorn and Brennus' families, too."

Brennus swallowed, staring at the floor. "They've

all disappeared."

Fedilmid thrummed his fingers together, elbows resting on his knees. "I see." He leaned back in the chair and crossed one leg over the other. "Your Aunt Moira must be very worried."

Guilt washed over Fable. She hadn't allowed herself to think too much about her aunt since she and Timothy had been transported through the book. She pictured Aunt Moira sitting at home, fretting over their disappearance. She imagined that Moira had called the police by now, and that they'd combed every inch of the woods behind Rose Cottage. Poor Grimm must be devastated at the loss of his children. Her heart ached when she thought of his sad, droopy face.

"Did you know her too?" Fable asked.

"I never met her, but I heard a lot of great things about her," Fedilmid replied, his voice soft and gentle. "She sounds like a kind—and brave—woman. They thought very highly of her."

"Aunt Moira? Brave?" Fable tilted her head. "She's the queen of safety."

Algar chuckled from the kitchen. He added the meat to a pot, along with the chopped vegetables. The savoury aroma of stew filled the small cottage, warm and comforting.

"I doubt raising two children on her own is an easy

141

feat," Fedilmid said with a kind smile. "I can't imagine the work of it even with a partner." He nodded his head towards Algar. "Much less on my own."

Fable blushed and glanced at her friends. Now they would know the full truth, that she was a thorn in her aunt's side. She thought about how hard Aunt Moira worked to make ends meet. But even though she worked long hours at her job, there was always a warm meal on the table for them. She never denied them help with their homework, or reading to them before bed, no matter how tired she was. Fable had never thought about what life must be like for Aunt Moira before.

"I guess. She does work hard for us. And she never really wanted me. I was forced on her when my parents died."

"Ah, I doubt that's the truth of it," Fedilmid replied. "If she didn't want you, I don't think you'd have a home at Rose Cottage."

Fable mulled over Fedilmid's words as she took another sip of tea. All her life, she had felt like a burden to her aunt. Life would have been easier on her aunt if it were just Moira and Timothy. Fable was an expense, and Aunt Moira's long hours at work were because she had two extra mouths to feed instead of one. And Fable was different—she had magic, and that was something dangerous, something Moira had to contain and cover up to the world.

But Fable remembered all the laughs, stories, and games they'd played together. The times her aunt had doctored her scrapes and bruises and kissed them better.

Maybe Fedilmid was right. Maybe Aunt Moira wanted her. She felt unsettled, guilty about the way she had often spoken to her aunt. And now she might never see her again.

Fedilmid broke the silence with his kind, gentle voice. "I am going to send a note to Moira that you're here, and safe."

Fable's attention snapped back to the room. "Please, no! I have to find Timothy first. She's going to freak out if she knows I lost him."

"You didn't lose him . . ."

"I did. It's my fault." Tears welled up behind Fable's eyes. "The book. I tried to destroy it with magic."

"What book, my dear?" Fedilmid asked.

Fable tossed the book bag to him. He caught it, opened it carefully, and slid out the grisly tome. He nearly dropped it when he saw the cover. "This pattern. Where did you get this book, child?"

The tears spilled out of her eyes and streamed down her face. Fable poured the whole story out to him. How the book fell from the shelf on its own, the nightmare

143

and the smoky tentacles that burned her wrists, and about her and Timothy's decision to destroy the book. She even shared her attempts at magic, and how they often blew up in her face. She told them that Moira thought she was dangerous.

"And I am. I lost Timothy. I have no idea where the book took him. He could be dead, for all I know."

Brennus had his head in his hands, his face hidden. Thorn wiped tears from her own eyes and pulled a handkerchief from the pocket of her burlap dress. She blew her nose loudly into it. Algar bowed his head over the stove and stirred the stew pot with a steady motion.

"Fable." Fedilmid rose, placing the book on the table beside his chair. He crouched down in front of her. His eyes, soft and caring, met hers. "This is not your fault. I don't know where this book is from, but it has far greater power than you know. Or had, anyways. It appears to be depleted now—I don't sense any more magic in it. It must have expelled all of its power when it transported you."

Fable hiccupped. "How am I going to get him back?"

Thorn spoke up. "You're not alone. We're in this together."

"Yeah," Brennus agreed. He put his arm around her shoulder. "We're not splitting up now. You've saved me twice. I think I owe you." He turned to Fedilmid. "And that's not all, sir. Thorn and I are tied up in this, too. Both our families vanished right after getting strange objects with that pattern on them."

He pointed at the book, then shared the story of his father's guitar. Thorn chimed in about her sister's bow.

After listening to their stories, Fedilmid sat back in his chair, his hand on his chin. He stared at his mug on the stand beside him. After a moment, he slapped his hand on his knee.

"Algar, is supper ready? Let's eat."

"Eat?" Fable asked. Her stomach, starving earlier, ached at the thought of a meal. She couldn't fathom forcing food into it now.

Algar ladled steaming stew into bowls.

"Good plan, Fedilmid. The mind can't work on an empty stomach." He smiled at the children and set the bowls down on the table. "Come on, kids, while it's hot."

"But—" Fable wanted to continue their discussion. She was dying to know what Fedilmid and Algar knew about the book, the pattern, and what it all meant. She was eager for long conversations about her parents and their pasts, and what Fedilmid knew about their deaths.

"Eat. We will discuss more later." Fedilmid strode to the table and sat in front of a hefty steaming bowl of rabbit stew. The children begrudgingly followed him. Thorn looked down at the soup, a frown on her face.

"Don't worry, kiddo," Algar said. He sat down across from her. "I left the rabbit out of yours. Potatoes, carrots, peas, and beans."

"How did you know?" Thorn asked.

"I had a Folkvar friend once. A long time ago, when I was young," Algar said. "I know your kind very well. Eat up."

A smile lit up Thorn's face, and they settled down to eat.

Fable's empty stomach gave in to the comforting smell of the stew in front of her, but her mind still raced. She hoped Timothy, wherever he was, had a good meal and a roof over his head, too.

Words from the Past

The old cuckoo clock on the wall over the mantle ticked the time away. Lying beside Thorn on a mat on the living room floor of the dark and quiet Tulip Manor, Fable rolled over again, trying to find a comfortable position. Her tired body craved sleep, but her mind wouldn't allow it. Brennus, on Thorn's other side, snorted and tugged at the quilt they were all sharing. Thorn snored peacefully, her toes sticking up beyond the lower edge of the quilt.

Fable couldn't believe she had met somebody who knew her parents. Cut off from the world in Larkmoor, she'd never dreamed that would happen. Her heart leapt at the thought that her parents had slept right here—in this very cottage, on this very floor.

She knew she'd been left safely behind with Aunt Moira when her parents went on their fateful journey. She wasn't with them when they met Fedilmid and Algar, but it was like she'd known the wizened men all her life. It was a strange feeling for her, to feel so safe and accepted.

Her mind wandered to Timothy. The only clue Fedilmid and Algar could provide about his disappearance was that they'd seen the image on the book before. When they had looked for Jinny Greentoes after she went missing, they'd found a broken teacup resting on her table with that exact design painted on it. The teapot was gone, a charred mark on the table where it must have rested. Fedilmid had been quite put off by it. He said he only remembered it so vividly because of how horrific it was.

"Why would anybody want such a terrible design on their fine china?" he said. He much preferred the snapdragon pattern on the vintage set he inherited from his grandmother. "Despite the scales and teeth, they're really quite lovely."

The only progress they made on the quest to find their families was Fedilmid's insistence on sending word to Moira. Algar firmly agreed.

"This isn't something you kids can do on your own," he said. "Moira is probably worried sick. She needs to know where you are and what's happened to Timothy. Once she arrives, then we'll make a plan."

Fable swallowed the lump in the back of her throat. She would have to face her aunt eventually, and maybe sooner was better. Finding Timothy was proving harder than she thought. *Besides, if Aunt Moira had helped me with my magic instead of forcing me to suppress it, we wouldn't be in this mess to begin with.* Maybe now her aunt would see that, and they could finally work together.

Fedilmid pulled some parchment from his robes. He laid it on the table, and Algar passed him a ballpoint pen from a cluttered shelf on the wall beside them.

He laid the pen on the table and, with a flick of his wrist, it jumped to attention. Fedilmid merely waved his hand in the air, and the pen danced across the page in fluid motion. Fable peeked over his shoulder to read the flourish of fancy lettering he used to sign it off.

Hope you are well in spite of these circumstances,

The Fey Witch, Fedilmid Coot of Tulip Manor in the Lichwood of Starfell

He folded it and stuffed it into an envelope and sealed the letter with red wax. He pressed one of his ornate rings into the wax, leaving the imprint of his initials, FC, in spirally letters.

In a few quick strides, Fedilmid was at the window above the kitchen sink. With a grand gesture, he wiggled his fingertips over the envelope in his other hand and murmured under his breath. Purple and green glitter flowed over the paper. He slid the window open and thrust the letter into the air. It floated, waiting for direction.

"To Moira Nuthatch, Rose Cottage in Larkmoor," Fedilmid instructed it. "If anyone but Moira tries to open you, you are to spontaneously combust immediately."

Fable had gasped in wonder as the letter had spun off into the air, vanishing into the night with a trail of glitter sparkling behind it.

Fable sighed. It was no use. She was wide awake. She rolled onto her side and noticed a pile of books under the side table next to her. She counted them, hoping it would ease her mind and lull her into sleep.

"Fifteen, sixteen, seventeen . . ." She lost count, distracted by a hardcover journal shoved into the middle of the stack of books on druidcraft and gardening.

It was a pretty notebook, covered in pink florals. Fable slid it out of the pile. She rubbed her fingers together and conjured a soft light in her palm. When she flipped the cover open to reveal the first page, the name "Faari Nuthatch" jumped out at her in pretty cursive letters. Her heart skipped a beat. Her mother. She must have forgotten it here all those years ago.

She rolled onto her stomach and rested the book on her pillow. She tried not to disturb the snoring Thorn as she carefully turned the page to reveal her mother's first entry.

For the next hour, Fable lay reading, entranced

by her mother's words. The soft light from her palm gently illuminated pages containing endearing stories of her father, tales of adventure and journeys through the mountains, and beautiful botanical sketches of herbs and flowers Faari collected along the way. Her heart ached. It was as though her mother came alive in these pages.

She kept reading until she came to the last page in the notebook. On it was sketched a rough outline of the viney design Fable had come to know so well. Beside the image, she read the words:

After spending several weeks at Tulip Manor and exploring Jinny's cottage, we are no closer to finding her or the answers we are looking for. I'm afraid she has met the same end as Morton's mother. There was a teacup in the kitchen bearing an identical design to Belinda's enchanted flower box. The teapot was nowhere to be seen. I'm convinced these items are portals, and that Endora has been using them to capture our loved ones.

My heart is broken. We should have stopped Endora for good years ago when we had the chance. I don't know how much time Jinny has left, or if she is even still alive. I don't know if we can get to her in time. Endora's mansion is much deeper into the Lichwood along the Shadow Walk Trail. However, since we might be Jinny's only hope, we have no choice but to leave tomorrow to try and save her. Fedilmid and Algar have graciously offered to accompany us, but I fear that they have no idea what we'll be up against. Endora is our responsibility, not theirs, and we couldn't bear to put them in danger. We are leaving at dawn to find her and face her ourselves. If we don't stop her now, many more people will be destroyed because of her greed.

Fable's stomach dropped, any notion of sleep now gone. They couldn't wait for Aunt Moira to arrive. Fedilmid's letter wouldn't even reach her until the next day, and Larkmoor was hundreds of miles from the Lichwood Forest. If her mother's words were true, they would never get to Timothy in time if they waited.

Fable didn't know what evil lurked down the Shadow Walk Trail, but they had to try. She closed the book, sat up, and shook Thorn's shoulders. They had to move out now.

Fiendish Fungi

Tulip Manor was draped in darkness. The moon hid behind a cloudy veil and the forest felt even more somber and silent than the day before. Fable never thought she'd long for the sounds of chirping insects or croaking toads, which were often loud enough to keep her awake at home. Now, the unnatural silence made the hair on the back of her neck stand up.

"You're sure this is the right way?" Brennus whispered. They crept alongside the treeline behind Tulip Manor. Fable stepped softly, hoping they wouldn't wake Fedilmid and Algar. Even Thorn, bringing up the rear, managed to slip quietly through the tall grass.

Fable pointed ahead of them. "There's the trail."

She shivered, despite wearing Thorn's cozy sweater over her dress for warmth. Safely slung over her shoulder underneath it was her book bag. Now, along with the *Book of Chaos*, the bag held the added weight of Faari's journal. The magical book may have lost its power, but Fable couldn't let go of the hope that it still held another clue.

The trio reached the opening into the forest and stopped at the head of the trail. A rough wooden sign was nailed to the tree.

Thorn squinted at the sign and cleared her throat loudly. "Shadow Walk Trail," she read to her friends. "Sounds about right." Her voice rang through the clearing.

Fable and Brennus froze where they stood. Fable held a finger up to her mouth and motioned for Thorn to be quiet. Straining to see the cottage in the dark, she held her breath and looked for any sign of movement. A few seconds later, when all remained still, she let the air out with a loud sigh.

"Ssh!" Brennus hissed at her.

Thorn shook her head and peered into the dark forest. Fable followed her gaze down the gloomy trail. A thick grey mist rolled over the ground.

Brennus looked at Fable. "We should wait."

Fable lifted her chin and stepped into the forest. Brennus sighed and followed her, and Thorn came after him. With the memory of the angry hounds in her mind, Fable listened for any sign of movement. There was nothing.

"It's really creepy in here," Thorn whispered loudly from the back. "I don't like it. My hairs are standing on end. That's never been good."

"Yeah, and she would know. She's got more hair than both of us combined," Brennus said.

Fable stopped and turned to them, her jaw set. "The quicker we get to Timothy, and your families, the better the chances are that they'll be alive."

Thorn and Brennus exchanged a look.

"Fine." Thorn sighed. Mist curled around her body. It was getting thicker.

Fable's face softened. "We'll find them. I have a feeling this Endora person is behind it all." Rubbing her palms together, she conjured a soft light.

A weak, high-pitched giggle cut through the night air. Brennus spun around, peering into the dark.

"Who's there?" he said.

The giggle rang out again. Fable jumped, and Thorn looked around blindly. "I can't see a thing!"

A child-like voice pierced through the darkness. "They think they're alone, don't they?"

"I believe they do, dear sister. Not that we would help them," a deeper, smoother voice replied.

"Show yourselves!" Brennus stomped off the trail through the fog.

"Down here! Don't step on me," the deeper of the two voices snapped.

Brennus squinted at the ground. He crouched and

parted the long grass to get a better look, and then he barked a laugh.

"You're mushrooms!"

Fable and Thorn relaxed and walked through the mist to join him. Fable squatted next to him, illuminating the area with her hand, and saw two red mushrooms with white spots splattered over their caps. They looked like a character in Timothy's video games. Her mouth fell open when one bent back, its cap craned towards the ground. Two beady little eyes peered up at them from its stem.

"Yes, we're mushrooms! What were you expecting? Dandelions?" The gills underneath the red cap rippled.

The smaller of the two bent its head up, as well. Its gills waved as another giggle filled the air.

"They can't hear them, can they?"

There was a prickling sensation on the back of Fable's neck. Whatever type of creature the little fungi were, they weren't friendly. A shiver ran up her spine as the deeper voice spoke again.

"No, I dare say they can't."

"What are you talking about?" Brennus asked. He prodded the larger mushroom with his finger.

"Ouch! Unhand me, sir!"

"I'd be running right about now if I were them."

Fable listened hard for the sound of footsteps

through the long grass. Thorn scanned the trees for any sign of movement. The shadow of her ax loomed over them. She looked fiercer than ever. In that moment, Fable felt relieved that she could call Thorn her friend.

Not that it did her any good, as her feet were knocked out from under her a second later. On her back in the grass, Fable watched Thorn heave her ax above her head and then swing it at a dark shadow. The Folkvar girl roared with anger, her eyes flashing yellow. Then the world went dark.

Trapped

Fable opened her eyes. She lay with her cheek pressed against a rough wooden floor that was scattered with straw. It lurched and her stomach rolled. The moon had come out. Black silhouettes of trees glided by beyond a set of iron bars. She groaned and shook her head to clear the fog from her mind.

She was in a cage. And that cage was moving down a trail.

She sat up and gingerly touched her lip, which was swollen. Her whole body ached.

Her books! She patted her sides, feeling for the book bag under her sweater. She found the hard, sharp edges of it and let out a sigh of relief. She still had her books, the only clues she and her friends had.

Beside her, Thorn sat leaning against the bars with her eyes closed, breathing deeply.

Brennus knelt on the other side of Fable, his body pressed up against the iron door. He had one hand through the bars fumbling with the lock, his jaw clenched.

Fable knelt forward to get a better look through the bars. Four wide hunched backs covered with bristled black hair swayed in two lines in front of them.

One of them grunted and slashed at the other's side with long razor-sharp tusks.

Boars. Enormous, smelly boars with tiny black eyes and gnarled, kinky tails.

The other hog squealed and slashed back at his companion. They butted the sides of their heads, snorting. One of the two tall hooded figures walking on either side of the beasts snapped a glowing blue whip above their heads. The two boars glared at each other but pointed their noses straight ahead again.

The other hooded swineherd also carried a glowing whip and had Thorn's great ax propped on its shoulder. Both of them stared straight ahead and moved with a stiff gait. Other than their reaction to the hogs' scuffle, they gave no hint of awareness of their surroundings.

"It's no use! I can't get it open." Brennus swung the lock with a clang against the bars. It remained securely closed around the latch. He turned and looked at Fable. His face was bruised, his left eye black and puffy. He held a multi-tool with a wooden handle, a long silver hooked end protruding from it. "This pick always works." He slid to the floor with sagging shoulders.

Fable stared at Brennus' swollen eye. "What happened to you?"

"Could ask you the same thing. You look awful."

Fable touched her face, feeling her split lip and the large goose egg on her forehead. Her hair was ragged and knotted, with mud crusted through her locks.

"What happened?" She rubbed at a piece of mud on her cheek.

"I think we were ambushed. The only thing I remember is that Thorn got thrown down by some

shadowy thing. Next thing I knew, I was lying in here."

Thorn opened her eyes, which were their usual murky green.

"I can't eat mushrooms anymore."

"What?" Brennus wrinkled his nose, smudged with dirt.

"Mushrooms," she said again. She turned her stony gaze to meet his. "I can still hear their voices. I've lost half my diet."

Brennus' gaze darted to Fable.

Fable patted Thorn's leg. "We'll find something else for you to eat. Let's worry about that later. Do you remember what happened?"

"Yeah." Thorn jerked her head towards the bleak forms who walked beside the boars. They moved in silence, either ignoring their prisoners or not hearing them at all.

"Those two jumped us. I don't know where they came from. I didn't hear a thing." Thorn clenched her fists. "After they knocked you two out, they turned on me. They're crafty, let me tell you. One caught my ax when I swung at it and tore it right from my hands. They kicked out my legs to get me down. I can't believe they beat me." She pounded a fist on her knee.

"Did they say where they're taking us?"

"No." Thorn replied. "They're weird. They haven't said a word, or even looked back here."

"They keep the hogs in line," Brennus said.

As if to prove Brennus' point, one boar jumped sideways, jerking his line-mates and the carriage. The figure beside it snapped the whip. The creature grunted and stepped back into its place.

The trees parted and the trail widened. Up ahead, a mansion loomed in the distance, surrounded by a tall, wrought-iron fence. Beyond the bars, topiary hedges trimmed into the shapes of demons and dragons jutted out through the mist that blanketed the perfectly groomed lawn. Fable eyed a bush trimmed into the shape of a gargoyle with its wings spread wide. She had the creepy sensation that it was watching them.

As they approached the fence, Fable noticed that

the gate was worked with wrought-iron vines. Vines with sagging leaves, tangling around one another. They looked eerily similar to the vines on her book.

"Do you guys know this place?"

Thorn shook her head. "I thought only the Fey Witch lived in the Lichwood."

Brennus drummed his fingers on his knee. "I've never seen any place like this. I wish I wasn't seeing it now." He swallowed, taking in the scenery with wide eyes.

Their carriage stopped in front of the gate. One of the two guards stepped up and murmured something Fable couldn't hear. With a loud grating noise, the gate swung open.

A freshly gravelled path lay before them. It led to the top of a hill, where a white stone mansion stood starkly against the night sky.

The guards snapped their whips above the boars' backs. With disgruntled squeals, the animals jerked the carriage forward. The strange group wound their way up towards the estate. The demonic-looking hedges that lined the driveway clawed at them through the fog. Brennus moved closer to Thorn's side.

Thorn nudged Fable with her elbow and nodded towards the mist. Fable followed her gaze and her heart stopped. Hulking, snarling four-legged creatures crept through the haze. One lunged at the boars, and Fable let out an involuntary squeak. A guard lashed out with its whip and the beast retreated with high-pitched yelps. It was one of the hounds that had chased them to Tulip Manor.

"There are tons of them," Brennus whispered.

Fable's breath caught in her throat. Dozens of canine shadows lurked in the mist, watching them with glowing red eyes. She wasn't sure which was worse— running through the forest being chased by those brutes or being stuck in this cage surrounded by them.

The carriage creaked to a stop at the front steps of the house. The hogs jostled each other, their feet crunching on the gravel beneath them. After a jerk of their bridles by the guards, they stood still.

Fable stared at the imposing structure. It looked like an estate house from one of her books on the shelf at home, but there were no signs of a happy family. The lawn and front steps were bleak and empty. It didn't have that welcoming, warm feeling shared by Rose Cottage or Tulip Manor. It was too perfect—too immaculate and clean. She and her friends exchanged frightened looks.

The front door burst open and a tall beautiful woman with deathly-pale skin and pinned-up black hair strode out to the top of the steps and put a hand on her hip.

She looked ready for a royal ball in a sparkly floor-length black gown and enough diamond jewellery to fill a vault. She also looked like she hadn't seen the sun in years. But her most striking features were her dark purple eyes.

A short man with a toad-like face wearing a tweed jacket shuffled after her, carrying the long train of the dress. The smell of rotting cabbage wafted down the steps.

Fable gazed at the woman in awe.

"Fable Nuthatch." The woman's powerful voice cut through the air. She had a wicked grin on her face. "I've been waiting so long to see you."

TWENTY

Endora

Fable gaped at the woman, frozen to the spot. She had no idea who this strange lady was. And how did she know Fable's name?

The woman took a step forward and then glared at her dumpy companion, who had dropped the train of her dress and was gazing at Fable and her friends.

"A-HEM!"

With a start and a mumbled apology, he scrambled to pick up the train again. Satisfied, she strutted down the steps to the carriage, heels clicking on the stone. The squat man focused on his hands.

She walked up to the bars and looked directly at Fable with a broad smile on her blood-red lips. "My name is Endora."

Fable flinched at the name. Endora's smile broadened, her white teeth shining brightly in the dark. "You do know my name. I'm surprised. I thought Moira would have erased your family tree."

She sashayed to the front of the wagon, where both

guards stood side by side. They swivelled to face her. Fable gasped and shrank back against Thorn's solid warmth. Brennus gulped.

Under the hoods of their black cloaks, skeletal faces with empty eye sockets stared blankly at Endora, waxy skin hanging loosely off their bones.

"Take our guests inside to the suite on the second floor," Endora said to the one on the left. She turned to the other and pointed at the boars. "You, get these beasts out of my sight."

She walked back up the steps towards the doorway and snapped her fingers. The carriage lock flipped open and the door swung wide. Brennus' jaw dropped.

"Fable, you will meet me for tea in the morning after a good night's sleep. I'm sure you need a rest as much as I do," Endora said over her shoulder before disappearing into the house.

When the dress tugged at his hands, her henchman hiccupped and scurried along behind her.

One of the guards approached the carriage. It reached a bony hand through the door and grabbed the front of Brennus' hooded sweatshirt.

"Hey! I—"

The guard yanked Brennus roughly from the cage and threw him onto the gravel. He landed on his knees and glared at the figure. The hand reached back into the cage for Fable and she recoiled, backing into Thorn.

Thorn grabbed its frail wrist and its head jerked in her direction.

"No." Thorn lunged toward the door and pushed the skeletal guard to the ground. Grinning, she looked down at Brennus.

"They're not so strong."

A rope of blue lightning snaked around Thorn's body and pulled tight. The guard stood up, holding the handle of the whip, which crackled with electricity. Thorn cried out, her voice echoing into the night. With two hands on the whip, the guard yanked Thorn out of the carriage. She hit the ground with a thud.

"Stop!"

Fable jumped from the wagon to Thorn's side, glowering at the guard. Brennus stood and squared off beside her.

The guard flicked its wrist, and the sparking tail of the whip recoiled back into the handle.

Fable sank to her knees beside her friend. "Thorn! Thorn, are you okay?" She clutched Thorn's arm.

With a groan, Thorn opened one eye. "I'm fine."

She grimaced, and her eyes flashed from green to yellow and back again. She sat up and took a big breath.

"I think I know how they beat you in the forest." Brennus frowned.

Thorn heaved herself up to a standing position, and Brennus helped Fable to her feet.

Without a word, the guard walked towards the house.

"Let's go," Thorn whispered, jerking her chin towards the gravel path.

Fable hesitated, debating whether they should run. She exchanged glances with Brennus, who pointed at the mist and made signs for chomping teeth with his hands.

The guard wagged the end of the whip in the air without a look back.

Fable sighed. If they were going to escape, it wouldn't be right now. With hounds surrounding the premises it was too dangerous. "I don't think we'll make it."

Brennus nodded, and they followed the grisly apparition. Thorn muttered under her breath but tailed them up the stairs.

When the group reached the front door, it swung open on its own. They stepped inside and found themselves in a long white hallway, dimly lit by ornate ebony chandeliers.

Portraits lined the walls, detailed paintings of people in elaborate frames covered in vine carvings. They were so intricate that it took Fable a moment to realize that they weren't actually photographs. Fable's breath caught in her throat as they walked down the hall. There was something curious about the paintings. The subjects varied from fierce-looking women in green cloaks, to knights in armour, to men with noses as pointy as their hats. On every face was the same sad, defeated expression.

"Hey." Thorn stopped. She gazed up at one of the portraits. The dim light in the hallway cast shadows across her worried face. "My parents."

"What?" Fable stepped to Thorn's side and looked up at the painting. Two adult Folkvars stared back at them. The female was clothed in a brown dress similar to Thorn's. She had the same long copper hair. Rather than wild and untamed, it was neatly braided down her back. One hand grasped her male companion's, her gaze directed toward their feet.

Her partner was broad-shouldered with brawny arms. He stared defiantly out of the portrait with blazing yellow eyes. A great ax like Thorn's rested over his shoulder.

"It's them." Thorn frowned. "Where did she get this?"

The guard reached the winding staircase at the end of the hallway. It turned around and shook the whip in its hand. Empty eye sockets bored down on them.

"We're coming," Fable muttered.

She grabbed Thorn's hand and led her away from the portrait. Brennus followed after them with an anxious look on his face. Fable hurried along, the thought of Thorn's body with the whip snaked around it floating through her mind.

When they entered the staircase, they plunged into darkness. The guard turned his wrist palm up and opened his fingers. A pale orange light shone from his hand. He started his ascent. Thorn cast one last glance back at her parents' portrait before she started to climb the stairs. Brennus followed her gaze, rubbed the back of his neck, and followed behind her.

Fable had lifted a foot onto the first step when a small movement from the portrait to her left caught her eye. She glanced at it, and her heart skipped a beat.

A familiar pale face stared out of the painting at her, his mouth stretched wide in a cry of terror, his arms shielding his face.

"Timothy!"

His gaze darted down to hers.

The picture is alive?

"Timothy?" She reached out a hand towards him.

He blinked.

"Fable!" Brennus' face appeared from around the corner of the stair landing. "It's shaking that whip again. You'd better come."

Fable lowered her hand. She couldn't believe it. Timothy was here. Trapped in a painting.

"I'll come back for you," she whispered.

Timothy blinked again.

With one last look, Fable turned and jogged up the stairs after Brennus.

"What held you up?" he whispered.

She pushed past him, and he had to jog a few steps to keep up with her until they rejoined the group. When they caught up, she turned to whisper over her shoulder.

"Timothy."

Brennus glanced at her out of the corner of his eye. He gave her a quick nod of understanding.

When they finally reached the top, they entered a hallway with doors lining either side. There were no portraits or art of any kind in this hallway. A layer of dust coated the floor. Nobody had been up here for a very long time.

The guard stopped in front of the third door on the left. It pulled out a key and unlocked the door, opened it, and ushered Fable and her friends inside a spacious furnished room with iron bars over the windows. The door slammed shut behind them, the key clicking in the lock once more.

Fable peeked through the keyhole and saw nothing but the barren wall on the other side.

She, Brennus and Thorn blinked at each other with stricken faces lit only by the silvery light of the moon shining through the bars.

How were they going to escape from this?

Tea for Two

When the sun rose a few hours later, Fable stirred and sat up, shaking her head to clear her exhaustion. She'd barely slept a wink, tossing and turning with the vision of Timothy's face in the painting—and his eyes, very much alive—burnt into her mind.

In the daylight, the room looked like it belonged to a luxury bed-and-breakfast—impeccable white walls, trimmed with black and white floral wallpaper, a king-sized bed with a down comforter that matched the design on the walls, and a sable velvet couch in front of a wood-panelled fireplace. If it weren't for the bars on the windows, she could almost imagine she'd fallen into a fairy tale.

She frowned. She'd take the floor of Tulip Manor over this any day.

Beside her in the bed, Thorn snored loudly into a pillow wet with drool.

Brennus stirred under a blanket on the couch across

the room.

Fable slid from the bed and looked down to see a long, white nightgown touching the floor. She didn't remember changing her clothes in the night, but her tattered yellow sundress and moss green sweater were nowhere to be seen.

Her eyes scanned the room for her book bag. Relief washed over her when she saw the familiar starry pattern lying on the chair next to Brennus. She walked over to it and untied it to peek inside. The two books lay innocently together, still there and still safe.

The door opened and in walked the short, broad man who served Endora. He wrung his hands together and bowed.

"M-mistress Endora will sees you now for tea."

"Now? Where are my clothes?" Fable tugged at the neck of the nightgown.

Thorn snorted loudly and murmured something about mushrooms. She rolled over in her sleep. The servant glanced at the Folkvar warily.

He looked at Fable, his watery eyes bulging. "Methinks you look very nice."

She looked down and realized her hand now tugged at black lace. The nightgown had disappeared, and in its in place was a sequined black dress with a tulle skirt that reached her knees. She turned a heel to admire the polished leather shoes on her feet.

"Oh."

She looked back at her sleeping friends. Swallowing her fear, she followed the servant out of the room. They walked down to the end of the hall and began to descend the stairs.

"What's your name?" Fable asked him.

He kept walking and looked straight ahead. "Why?"

"How will I know what to call you if I don't know your name?"

He stopped and turned to study her. He was really very short—at least a full head shorter than her, though about twice as wide. His mouth twitched.

"Arame."

"Nice to meet you, Arame." She held out her hand.

Arame hesitated, looking at her outstretched fingers as if they were about to bite him. She wiggled them, and a smile crept over his face. He took her hand, gave it two quick pumps and turned back to the stairs.

They rounded the corner down onto the main floor. At the foot of the stairs, in the same spot as the day before, hung Timothy's painting. Fable gave him a quick glance and averted her eyes.

Arame led her to the French doors at the end of the hallway—white with black trim, like the rest of the house. Fable swallowed the prickly feeling that crept up her throat. Endora was in there. Waiting for her.

Arame bowed and held the door open. Fable stepped into a spotless kitchen.

Seated on one of two ornate chairs at a small round table in the breakfast nook was Endora. She had a smug smile on her face as she leaned over a delicate teacup—a cup that Fable thought must match Jinny Greentoes' teapot, with black vines painted along the rim and down the fine handle. Another dainty cup sat on a matching saucer, filled to the rim with brown liquid. A tin candy box sat in the middle of the table.

Endora wore another slim-fitting black gown with high, pointed shoulders that reached her ears. Her black hair was pulled back into a severe twist, and diamonds dangled from her earlobes.

"Good morning, Fable." She motioned for Fable to sit in the empty chair.

Fable walked across the room and gingerly took her seat. The tulle of her skirt poofed up around her, and she smoothed it as best as she could.

She eyed the tea and wondered what kind of magic lay in that cup. Something horrible, no doubt. Her gaze flicked up to meet Endora's. Amethyst irises, the same as her own, stared back at her.

Endora took a sip of her tea. Her red-stained lips didn't leave any trace on the white china.

"Did you sleep well?"

Fable nodded.

Endora set down her tea. She placed her elbows on the table and tucked her hands under her chin. "You're lying, Fable." Her purple eyes darkened. "I won't have that in my house. Next time, there will be consequences."

Fable swallowed, her eyes wide.

Endora leaned back in her chair with a self-satisfied smirk. "You don't know who I am, do you?"

"You're Endora," Fable said. "You killed Jinny Greentoes."

Fable's teacup flipped over, spilling hot liquid over the table and down onto her dress. It soaked through the fabric and burned her legs. Fable jumped, wiping her hands at the tea.

Endora shook her head with a sarcastic pout. "Tut-tut. I said there would be consequences for lies, child."

She stood up and leaned forward over the table as far as she could. Her face rested inches from Fable's. Fable flinched. She fought the urge to flee the kitchen and never look back.

Endora pinned Fable with an intense stare. "I am Endora Nuthatch, your great-grandmother."

A wave of defiance burned through Fable's chest. "You're not."

Her chair began to quiver beneath her. Something cold and sticky wrapped around her ankle, stinging her leg. She took a deep breath. *Be brave for Timothy.* If he could survive being trapped in that frame, she could deal with a tea party with a nasty hag.

She scowled at Endora. "You don't look old enough."

Her chair stopped shaking at once. She felt the cold slime shrink back down her leg and melt away.

"Oh, child." Endora's face lit up. Preening herself, she fluttered her hands. "I can forgive you for that. How shocking it must be to find out that your great-grandmother is so beautiful."

Fable let out a breath. Out of the corner of her eye she saw Arame, who was standing near the doorway, cover his mouth to hide his grin.

"How do you know me?"

"I've been watching you for years, dear," Endora replied. "When that wretched Moira stole you away to Larkmoor, I wanted to keep tabs on you. I know you're special. I know you have magic."

She took another sip of her tea. "My brand of power doesn't work in Larkmoor. They have enchantments that stop the darkest kinds of magic there. But I found a way to teleport into your room and plant my Collector on your bookshelf."

She wrapped her hands around the cup and looked wistfully out the window of the nook. "I watched you grow through that book. I saw your powers building." Hunger flashed in her eyes.

"But when I tried to bring you here, I got that blasted boy instead." Endora wrinkled her nose. "Useless child. The book was meant to pull only one soul into that portrait. Yours. Something that small can't handle two. And now it's unusable. My masterpiece, wasted." She paused, lost in thought.

"I figured it spit you out somewhere near the Lichwood. I sent my hounds and guards to hunt you down."

"So, you kidnapped both me and Timothy." Fable sat up straight in her chair. Under the table, she clenched her fists on her knees. "What did you do to him?"

Endora ignored her. She popped open the treat tin on the table. Wriggling worms and beetles squirmed inside it. Fable's stomach lurched. Endora reached in and plucked a beetle between her claw-like fingers. She held the thrashing insect up for inspection and then popped it into her mouth with a crunch.

"Cricket?"

Fable felt faint. She shook her head. Endora shrugged and helped herself to another squirming treat.

"I am a powerful sorceress." Endora licked her lips

179

and folded her hands on the table. "I can steal years and add them to my life. Oh, there are drawbacks— I've had to deal with so much jealousy. But it's worth it." She sighed loudly, clearly enjoying the sound of her own voice.

"I look in the mirror and see such perfection smiling back at me. And you, Fable, if you stay here and join me, you, too, can share in all of this." She waved her arm around the kitchen. "Beauty, wealth, power—"

"Power?"

"Oh, yes, dear." Endora grinned. "When you have magic as strong as ours, people fear you. And that fear gives you power. You haven't tapped into the darkness yet, but I can sense it in you. I feel it flowing through your veins. You see, the same power runs through mine. You are blessed. You are the only Nuthatch after me who was born with that power."

Fable looked down at her hands. She thought about all the times her magic had backfired. She remembered her life in Larkmoor, hiding herself from the world. She thought of Aunt Moira's solitary life, and how she'd barricaded them in Rose Cottage. She shook her head.

"Life is lonely when people fear you."

"Nonsense, child." Endora's voice was sharp. "I am surrounded by those who worship me. They abide by my every command."

"They don't even speak," Fable said.

"Of course they don't speak. They're dead." Endora slapped her hand down on the table. "If not for me, they'd be lying in the dirt. Nothing more than worm food."

"What?" Fable slid her chair back as she recoiled from the table.

Endora threw her head back and cackled. "What did you think? That they weren't moisturizing enough? They're dead. I raised them from their dank holes in the earth. In turn, they serve me."

Arame croaked loudly. He fiddled with the bow tie around his thick neck.

"Ah, except for him." Endora waved a hand in his direction. "Arame is very much alive. But he serves me for other compelling reasons."

Fable felt sick.

"Well, what do you say, child?" Endora asked. "Return home to that boring, non-magical town? Or stay here with me, living in splendour? Learning your craft, gaining power and beauty forever?"

"I'd like to go lay down."

"What?"

"I'd like to go lay down," Fable repeated.

Endora tapped her long red fingernails on the table and glowered at Fable. The clock on the wall ticked away the seconds.

"I'll give you today to think on it," she finally said. She stood. "No meals, and no leaving your room. For you or your friends. Arame, see Fable to her room. I'll be in my library."

She stalked to the door of the kitchen, then glanced back over her shoulder at Fable, eyes narrowed.

"You have until breakfast tomorrow."

The door swung open of its own accord and she was gone.

Fable threw a dirty look after her. *Until breakfast tomorrow? I have that long to break us out of here.*

Arame shuffled in his spot by the door.

"Could you show me her library?" Fable asked.

"No." He motioned for her to rise.

She stood up from her chair and met him at the door. "I could help you, too," she whispered.

He hesitated, regarding her with a pained expression on his face, then opened the door and walked out of the kitchen.

Fable trailed along behind him and gazed up at the sad, down-turned faces on the wall. She wondered if all these people inside the portraits were trapped, too. Maybe Thorn's parents were still alive. If Fable could find a way to free Timothy, perhaps she could find a way to get them all out.

She stopped at Timothy's painting at the base of the stairs. Timothy's eyes met hers, his face still frozen in his silent scream. Fable reached out and touched the glass. Timothy blinked twice, and his lip twitched as if he were trying to speak.

"Ahem." Arame cleared his throat. He stood partway up the steps, facing her.

Fable snapped her hand back. Tears stung her eyes. Arame's expression softened and he glanced at Timothy's portrait.

"That one's still there," he said. "When they stops moving, that's when you know they is gone."

"Arame . . ." she began, a lump in her throat.

With a sigh, he reached out a hand to her. "Here," he said. His face was soft, his bulbous eyes wide and earnest.

Fable took a step forward and clasped his hand. As her fingers touched his, he croaked. A long slimy pink tongue flicked out from his lips and licked his left eye.

Horrified, she tried to pull her hand away, but it was too late. The floor rocked beneath her and the hallway vanished.

TWENTY-TWO

The Magic and Lore of Starfell

Fable tried to scream. A rubbery webbed hand clamped over her mouth and muffled it. Arame's pleading face stared at her through the bar of light shining through the crack in what appeared to be a closet door. He held up his finger over his lips. Fable nodded, her heart hammering in her chest, and he removed his hand from her face.

They stood in a tidy walk-in closet used for storage. A table at the back held glass jars filled with insects and indistinct objects that floated in various colours of liquid, glinting slightly in the feeble light. A cast-iron cauldron sat in the corner beside a stack of boxes.

"Don't moves. Be quiet," Arame whispered. With a flick of his long tongue, he was gone.

Fable peered through the wooden slats of the door. Shelves filled with books lined the room on the other side. Endora's library.

Fable squinted, reading a few of the titles. There were books on fashion, some historical memoirs, and quite a few modern romances. Other volumes were a bit more tattered, a little grimier, and a lot more frightening. *How to Steal a Maiden's Beauty—Teeth, Skin and Hair. Re-Using Old Graves.* And, most alarming of all, *101 Ways to Suck the Life out of Your Enemies.*

Straight across from the closet stood an orderly claw-footed desk. Bent over it, in all her terrible splendour, was Endora. She pored over an open book that lay in front of her, blood-red lips pursed and brow furrowed.

Behind her on the wall hung a mirror between two life-sized, full-length portraits. One frame contained a haggard old woman with a kerchief on her head. In the other was a knight.

The knight pounded on the glass with metal-clad fists. Fable stifled a gasp. His arms reached back over his head as he landed blow after blow, but the glass didn't give any sign of weakness. Not even a crack. She thought of Timothy, frozen in the frame at the foot of the stairs. If that knight couldn't break the glass, how would she?

The door from the hallway cracked open. Arame poked his head in. "M-mistress?"

Endora raised her head. "Yes, Arame?"

He opened the door wider and slunk into the room.

185

He bowed his head.

"I was just wondering . . . what do you wants me to do with the other childrens?"

"Put them into frames," Endora said with a dismissive flick of her wrist.

Arame nodded, and his Adam's apple bobbed.

The sorceress faced the mirror on the wall between the two portraits. She pinched at her cheek and scowled as her skin sagged slightly in response, appearing to melt. "My face isn't holding like it used to."

Keeping her eyes trained on her reflection, she snapped her fingers imperiously. The knight fell to his knees, writhing in pain. Endora, eyes closed, breathed in deeply and smoothed her hand over her face. Her skin immediately regained a youthful glow.

"That's better." She smirked into the mirror then walked back to her desk. "I have more frames hanging on the third floor. The Folkvar girl's parents are on the wall here somewhere. They were rich with energy. They gave the bounce back to my luscious hair." She chuckled softly. "With the young one, I'll have the whole set."

"I think its sister's out there still." Arame indicated the outside world with an encompassing wave of his hand.

Endora traced her finger over the page in front of

her. "Shame. We'll find her. Once I gain enough power to leave this wretched house again."

"It can't be much longers, mistress." Arame began to tidy one of the book shelves. "We're only a few months off from the girl-child's thirteenth birthday."

"Yes." Endora's amethyst eyes flashed. She licked her pointer finger and turned the page. "The timing is right. She'll soon come into her full powers. I've been waiting years for this. According to this book," she tapped it with a pointy red nail, "her birthday lands on the day that the Blood Star will fall. And if I should find that star . . ."

"And puts it with the girl-child's blood . . ." Arame prompted.

"I will absorb her power." She closed the hardbound book with a snap. "I will finally be able to leave this prison with my powers intact and establish my reign over the rest of Starfell." She tapped her fingers together in front of her face, her smile brighter than the wicked gleam in her eye.

Fable's legs felt like rubber. She struggled to keep herself from collapsing. Aunt Moira's constant fear and hiding away from the world in Larkmoor—finally it all made sense. She squeezed her eyes shut as shame washed over her. Shame for the way she had treated her aunt, for the way she had rebelled against her. No wonder Moira feared her magic.

Endora yawned and arched her back. "I'm ready for my siesta, Arame. Go. Run me a hot bath, and make sure you warm my towels."

He bowed to her and slipped from the room. Endora stepped in front of the mirror and preened at herself like a haughty black cat. "You're so close. Soon you'll have everything you've ever wanted. Everything you deserve."

She left the room with a flap of her glittering gown.

Fable waited a few moments, not daring to breathe for fear of Endora's return. When she was sure that Endora wasn't coming back, she quietly opened the door of the closet and stepped into the library. She listened for the clicking of Endora's heels in the hallway, but the room was quiet.

Fable approached the ebony desk and glanced at the knight's portrait. He was still on his knees, head down. His shoulders shuddered with every breath. She gently tapped the glass of his painting.

"Are you okay?"

He gave no indication of hearing her.

"I'll try to get you out, too."

She looked down at the book Endora had left on the desk. It was heavy, even bigger than the encyclopedia at home that Aunt Moira treasured. An intricate gold trim edged the black leather cover and balanced the title scrawled across it in golden letters.

"The Magic and Lore of Starfell," Fable read aloud.

She reached out to open the front cover. Green, sticky fingers closed over her wrist.

Arame.

"We haves to go," he said. "She wants me to captures your friends for the frames. Tonight. You must gets them and gets out." With that, Arame licked his eyeball and transported them out of the library.

TWENTY-THREE

The Galaxy Under the Floor

"I'm starving." Fable rummaged through the contents of Thorn's backpack, which lay strewn across the bed. She picked up a carrot, wiped it clean on her dress, and bit into it with a satisfying crunch.

Thorn, standing beside her, reached down and found a parsnip, still dirty from the earth it had been torn from. She rubbed it on her dress and popped it into her mouth, then picked up another and tossed it to Brennus.

The lanky boy had been sitting with his arms crossed in the overstuffed armchair by the fireplace. He caught the parsnip and looked at it with disdain. "Better than nothing, I guess. I can't believe she didn't even feed us."

They hadn't eaten since last night at Tulip Manor. Since Endora had locked them in, the only person they had seen was Arame. No guard had even checked up on them, much less delivered them food.

When Fable had popped back into the room beside

190

the hearth with Arame clutching her hand, Thorn had been pacing in front of it. She rushed at Arame and took a swing at his broad, flat head. With a disgruntled croak, he disappeared just in time for Thorn's fists to pummel the air where he'd stood moments before. Now, Brennus sat near that very spot, inspecting his parsnip as though it might bite him instead of the other way around, absorbing the news Fable had just shared.

"That crazy lady's your great-grandma?" Brennus asked Fable. He sniffed his parsnip, then took a bite.

Fable picked up a tent peg and eyed it. "So she says."

"That explains a lot," Brennus said with his mouth full. "The book, your aunt's behaviour, your magic."

Fable didn't respond. She regarded the supplies and handed the tent peg to Thorn, who shoved it into her backpack. "Are you guys sure you're okay with the plan?"

"Considering the only other option right now is death, yeah." Brennus rummaged through his pockets. His hand emerged holding his multi-tool. He flicked it, and the lock pick sprang out of the wooden handle. He pointed it at the key-hole lock in the door. "Step one, get out of here before the guards come."

Fable nodded. "Step two, get Timothy and Thorn's parents. Or at least their portraits." She didn't have the heart to tell Thorn what Arame had told her about the portrait's subjects. Despite what he said about them being gone once they stopped moving, she couldn't help but hope he was wrong.

Thorn zipped the leftover apples into the side pocket of her backpack. "Step three, get back to Tulip Manor and get help for the other poor souls trapped here. Easy-peasy."

Brennus twirled his lock pick in his fingers and glanced up at Fable, his brow furrowed. "You know we won't be able to just stroll out of here."

She fought back the butterflies in her chest. "If we leave before the guards know we're gone, I think we stand a chance. And Arame seems willing to help. Maybe he could zap us out of here." He was the only lifeline they had at the moment.

Fable picked up her book bag and slung it over her shoulder. She tugged at her dress, the tulle skirt rustling in her hands. Not exactly adventure wear, but she had no idea where her regular clothes had gone. It would have to do.

Having packed the backpack to her satisfaction, Thorn hoisted it onto her back and fastened the straps around her waist.

"Ready?"

"I hope this thing works." Brennus knelt in front of the door and began to work at the lock, frowning in concentration.

Fable held her breath. She hoped that Endora had underestimated them and that she hadn't magicked the door.

"Aha!"

The door clicked. Brennus grinned triumphantly and stood up, pulling it open towards them.

"Ladies first." He bowed.

Fable stepped past him to the threshold and peered into the still, dark hallway. There were no signs of any guards, or of Arame, or of any life at all. Her mouth went dry and her heart caught in her throat. It shouldn't be this simple.

She turned back to her friends and Thorn placed a hand on her shoulder. She pushed Fable aside, chuckling.

"Way too easy."

As she raised a foot to step into the hallway, the floorboards crumbled and fell away. They cracked and groaned as they broke from the threshold and disappeared into the darkness.

Thorn gazed into the hole with an open mouth. "Oh!" She teetered on the edge of the doorway, trying to catch her balance.

"Thorn!"

Fable and Brennus took hold of her burlap dress and pulled her back into the room. Thorn lost her footing and they toppled over backwards from her weight. The three of them landed in a pile on the floor.

Thorn sat up and rubbed her head. "What the heck was that?"

Fable untangled herself from the pile of limbs, both human and hairy, and walked to the doorway to inspect the mysterious hole.

One would think that a hole in the floor would open to the room below it, but this hole was different. This hole opened into an endless galaxy. It was filled with stars and planets and beautiful, swirling pink-and-blue dust clouds. Fable felt dizzy. She took a step back into the room and bumped into her friends. Brennus peered over her shoulder.

"Well, that's one way to keep us in here."

He took one of the parsnips Thorn had given him and tossed it down into the galaxy. It landed where the floor should have been and rested there for a moment. Then, with a small *pop* and a shimmer of ripples, it disappeared into the solar system below.

"I've never seen magic like that." Brennus stared at the galaxy in awe.

Thorn shuddered. "Thanks for pulling me back."

A shooting star sped across the sky beneath them. Fable wondered where it was going—where it was that stars hurried off to when they plucked themselves out of their bright spots in the sky. She watched in fascination, curious as to what types of life were on the planets below.

Brennus' voice pull her attention back to the problem at hand. "The window's barred. We have to find a way across."

"Would be nice if Arame showed up about now." Thorn sighed as she peered into the hallway.

"Can you use your magic?" Brennus asked Fable. "You know. Make us fly, or something."

Fable pursed her lips. "I don't know. I made my dog levitate once, but that was by accident. I don't even know how I did it."

Brennus tossed a potato out into the hallway. It hit the galaxy with a plop and sunk down into it. Once again, ripples glittered and spread across the atmosphere below them.

"Hey!" Thorn gave him a sharp look. "You're

tossing away our supper."

Fable caught his eye, and from the grin on his face she knew he'd had the same realization. "There's a surface," she said. "Quick, we need something that floats."

Brennus walked back into the room and took a piece of kindling from the wood box by the hearth. Quickly, he stepped back to the threshold and laid the thin piece of wood gently on top of the invisible surface. It floated. He looked up at Fable with a grin.

"Can you use your magic to conjure a boat? Or maybe a raft?"

"No, I've never even tried something like that." Her face grew hot. "I'm not very good, am I?"

"I believe in you." Thorn looked at Fable earnestly and placed a calloused hand gently on her shoulder.

Fable reached up and squeezed it.

She looked at the open oak door, and an idea crept into her mind.

"The door!"

Her friends followed her gaze, and Brennus grinned.

"I can get it down."

He walked over to the door and pried at the bottom hinge with his tool. It didn't budge.

Thorn snorted and stomped over to the door, stretching her arms over Brennus' head. She grabbed it with two hands, squatted down and gave a fierce heave upwards. Veins popped from her neck as the door jamb splintered and broke. With a loud *crack*, the door ripped from its hinges. Thorn stumbled backwards with it, knocking Brennus to the ground. Her chest heaved from the effort. She beamed at them.

Brennus, scowling, got to his feet and pocketed his pick. He dusted off his pants. "I almost had it."

Thorn looked sideways at him and raised a brow. The corner of her mouth quivered with restrained laughter. Brennus' face softened and he started to laugh. Fable grinned at her friends. A warm feeling of hope settled over her.

She gestured towards the door in Thorn's hands. "Let's see if it floats."

Thorn turned and dropped the door on top of the liquid floor. As Fable had expected, it hit with a splash. It rocked a few times, sending out ripples all the way to the end of the hallway, and then floated above the open expanse of stars.

"Do you think it'll hold all three of us?" Brennus asked.

"Or even just me?" Thorn scratched her head

197

through her wild, copper hair.

Fable looked at Thorn with fresh eyes. The Folkvar towered over her friends. Her size had never seemed so foreboding. Before, her large frame had been a comfort, a buffer in an unknown world of chaos. Now, for the first time, it might hold them back.

"I'll try making it stronger, just in case," Fable said.

She wasn't sure what she was doing, or if it would work, but she closed her eyes and placed her hands on the door. With every ounce of her being, she willed it to strengthen and the liquid below to hold. She cracked one eye open and saw a purple glow flow from her hands over the makeshift raft and absorb into the wood.

Fable crouched down and spread her hands wide on the door to steady it, feet still on the floor of the bedroom. She pressed on it to test its stability. Once she was sure it would hold, she crawled the rest of the way onto the board. It rocked a little but stayed afloat on the crystal-clear liquid.

"I think it's okay. Thorn, if you sit in the middle, I think it'll stay balanced." Fable beckoned for her friends to climb on.

Thorn knelt down and shimmied onto the door. It

lurched and sent waves rippling into space. Fable's hands gripped the sides to steady herself, and the door settled back down into a gentle rocking motion. Thorn sat sideways in the middle, knees bent up to her chest. Her toes hung over the side, but she was on it securely.

Brennus cleared his throat. He stood frozen at the edge of the doorway, staring into the depths of the universe below. His face was ghostly pale. "I—I can't . . ."

"Yes, you can." Fable peered at him around Thorn's elbow. "It's ok. We're here. We'll help you."

He didn't move.

Thorn turned her shoulders slightly and held out a big bluish-grey hand towards him. "Don't look down. Just look at us."

Brennus swallowed and looked directly into Thorn's eyes.

"You got this," Thorn said.

With a quick movement, Brennus grabbed her hand and dashed onto the door. He scooted up close to her and linked his arm with hers. The door pitched slightly from the impact but remained floating.

Fable looked along the hallway, trying to see where the gaping hole ended. The glow of the solar system beneath them provided gentle illumination to the otherwise-dark space. She could see the outline of the solid top stair against the luminous glow of a bright shining blue star below it. Now, how were they going to get over there?

Cautiously, she dipped the edge of her dress over the side of the door. It soaked up the clear liquid. She pulled it out and felt it with her hand. It was cold and wet.

"Well, it doesn't burn . . ."

She dipped one finger into it. Nothing happened. No monster lurked beneath to grab her, nothing stung her or capsized their little raft. She stuck her whole hand in, and, with all her might, she willed a small current to pick up and push them towards the stairs. The water rippled outwards from her hand, sending waves of soft purple and blue light glimmering into the galaxy below.

The door began to move. It slowly glided through the water over the constellations. The children hardly dared to breath. Thorn wrapped an arm around each of her friends, holding them close. With one hand in the water and one gripping Thorn's forearm around her middle, Fable willed their little raft along.

With a soft *thunk*, the door hit the edge of the top

step. Brennus grabbed the boards and swung the door lengthwise beside it. He patted the stair. It stayed solid under his hand.

"I think it's safe." He whispered. He stood and hopped over to the solid ground.

Thorn helped Fable over next, and then scrambled off the door herself. She grinned down at her smaller companions.

"That was amazing."

Brennus chuckled and ran a hand through his jet-black hair. The tulle of Fable's dress was scrunched up around her thighs from their ride. She smoothed it down and righted her book bag around her.

Staring into the darkness beyond, Fable rubbed her fingers together, and a soft light illuminated her palm. She glanced at her friends and took a tentative step into the stairwell.

Making History

F able and Brennus crept quietly down the stairs. Thorn tried to imitate their soft footsteps, without success. Fable cringed at her friend's thumping, but there was no time to slow down.

They didn't come across anybody in the dark stairwell. No guards, and no Arame. Fable let go of her hope that they would get Timothy's portrait, Arame would find them, and they would just teleport away. That would be too easy.

They reached the landing that would take them the final few steps to the hallway on the main floor. Fable stopped on the last step before the landing. Brennus bumped into her from behind, then Thorn jostled into him, and he let out an involuntary yell.

Fable twisted to look at them and put her finger to her lips. "Ssh!"

"It's Thorn's fault. Her and her big, clumsy feet," Brennus whispered.

Thorn grunted. "I think the real problem is you and

your big, loud mouth."

Fable shushed them again and peeked her head around the corner. The hallway was quiet, with only a few lights on the chandeliers to illuminate it. Fable closed her hand and the light in her palm went out. She crept down the last few steps into the open hallway, her friends following. She stood in front of Timothy's painting and looked up at him.

Her cousin's gaze flicked down to meet hers, his mouth still open wide in fear. Fable studied the familiar vines climbing up the frame around the emerald green canvas behind him. She reached up and touched the portrait. Her fingers slid over the smooth glass, unable to reach him.

"What do I do?"

Thorn and Brennus came to stand beside Fable.

"Now what?" Brennus squinted up at Timothy.

Thorn reached over Fable's head and grabbed the frame on each side. She tried pulling on it and pushing it side to side. It didn't so much as tilt from its place on the wall.

"Argh! It won't budge."

Timothy's gaze met Fable's again, and then darted away. She frowned and followed his gaze with her own. Down the hallway, towards the entrance. What was down there? Her gaze stopped at the big mahogany door halfway down the hall.

Understanding dawned on her. "The library."

Timothy glanced down at her again and gave a long, deliberate blink.

She turned away from him and hurried to the library door, then grabbed the iron knob. It wouldn't turn. Using all her strength, she twisted it both ways. It was no use. She took a step back and surveyed the door. Then she remembered a trick she'd used to sneak out and practice magic in the garden on nights when Aunt Moira had locked up the cottage, assuming that Fable slept soundly in her bed. Hoping it wouldn't set off her magic in another chaotic burst, she decided to give it a try.

With her hand on the doorknob, Fable closed her eyes and envisioned the lock inside sliding open. The knob grew hotter as the energy coursed into it from her hand. When it became so hot that she thought she couldn't hold onto it any longer, the energy fizzled and a green sheen flashed over the door. Cold bit into her hand from the freezing knob. She jerked it back.

"She's bewitched it." Fable rubbed her hand. She glared at the door. "She knew I'd try to get in here. There's got to be another way."

"What about the vent?" Thorn pointed up at the duct above the door. "I can't fit, but you two might."

Fable looked up. *Hmm . . .*

"Brennus, do you think you could open it?"

He squinted at it and scratched his head. "If Thorn holds me up there, sure."

"I'll keep watch for the guards."

Fable glanced down the hallway. Her back tingled as she stared at the portraits lining the walls. The people in them seemed to watch the three children. She wasn't sure if the prisoners were cheering them on or waiting for disaster to strike. She looked back over her shoulder to check Brennus' progress.

"Ready?" Brennus said to Thorn. He took his multi-tool out of his pocket and, with a flick of his fingers, a screwdriver popped out from the handle.

Thorn gave it an admiring gaze.

"Pretty handy, hey? My dad gave it to me. See? Here's his initials." He pointed to the roughly carved BT in the wood. "He used it dozens of times to break into old buildings."

Thorn's expression turned to a disapproving frown and he closed his mouth. Fable covered her smile with her hand.

Brennus flashed a scowl in her direction, then

tapped Thorn on the arm. "Anyway, boost me up. I'll have that vent open in no time."

Thorn bent down and cupped her hands together like a stirrup on a saddle. Brennus stepped into them with both feet and gripped her shoulders for balance as she stood. From there, he was able to reach the vent.

As he worked, Fable kept watch down the dimly lit hallway. Her heart hammered in her chest and the hairs on her arms prickled. She had visions of guards rushing into the hallway and Endora's heels clicking towards them.

"Grab it, Fable!" Brennus whispered loudly, snapping her back to reality.

He had the vent in one hand and was lowering it down to her. Fable took it and leaned it up against the wall.

"How does it look?" Thorn asked.

Brennus knocked on the inside of the vent with his knuckles. "It's solid, but I can't see much. Fable, you could use your glowy hand spell. What do you think? Are we going in?"

"I should go alone."

"I'm coming. You aren't going in there by yourself."

"Brennus." Fable shook her head.

"My family's missing, too." His jaw locked with

determination. He wasn't going to back down without a fight.

She relented with a sigh. "At least let me go first."

Thorn lowered Brennus back to the ground. She looked uneasily at Fable and scratched her elbow as she spoke.

"What if Endora's in there?"

Fable swallowed. "She'd have heard us by now."

She refused to think otherwise. She didn't have much choice. They'd gotten this far. There was no going back now.

Thorn reached out and pulled Fable toward her. She crushed her against her broad chest. "You're the bravest girl I know."

Fable hugged her back. "I wish I were as strong as you."

"You two are gross. Come on." Brennus rolled his eyes.

Thorn let go of Fable and set her jaw. "I'll keep watch. Don't be too long."

Thorn grabbed Fable around the waist and lifted her up to the vent, craning her neck and blowing at the smothering black tulle of her skirt. Using her elbows, Fable pulled herself inside and scooted further to make room for Brennus. She reignited her palm, and the light cast an eerie glow inside the vent as it reflected off the metal. Her knees rested in years of grime and dust, and the air smelled stale.

She heard Thorn heave Brennus up. He scrambled forward and plowed into Fable, pushing her into the side of the vent.

"Brennus!" Fable pushed his shoulder away from her face.

"Ah, sorry." He grinned sheepishly and forced himself backwards with his hands.

Fable held her shining hand in front of her and began to crawl towards the other end of the duct. Her heart pounded. She wasn't sure if her mind was playing tricks on her or if she actually heard faint scurrying noises ahead of them. *Rats.* She didn't want to think of what else might lurk in these dusty old vents. Brennus scuffled along behind her.

A few feet ahead of them, the slats of an opening came into view. She closed her palm, snuffing out her light.

Not much further.

She crept forward, probing with her fingers for the edge of the opening. Once she reached it, she peered down through the slats.

The shapes of bookcases loomed in the dark room.

The library. She tuned out the scurrying sounds from inside the duct and listened closely. There was only silence from below.

Squeezing herself tightly against the side of the vent, she motioned to Brennus, who slid up past her and took her place. He pulled out his pliers and set to work unscrewing the grate by gripping and twisting the pointy ends of the screws that poked through it from below. Fable held her breath at the squeaking noises the screws made when he whirled them out of their holes. There was a sharp bang when he popped the grate out of place. They stared at each other, not breathing, as they waited for any sign of a reaction below.

Silence.

Brennus shrugged his shoulders and moved toward the opening. Fable grabbed his sweater and motioned for him to stay put, squeezing past him. She closed her eyes and gathered up all the courage she had. Pushing every thought from her mind, she swung her feet down through the hole, then let go of the edge of the vent.

She landed on her side with a muffled cry. Her heavy bag thumped down onto her, and the corners of the books dug into her side.

Not daring to get up, she listened. There were no sounds of footsteps, or voices, or surprised gasps. But when she focused, she could hear a faint scratching sound. It came from the direction of Endora's desk. Fable squinted at the desktop, but all she could see on it was *The Magic and Lore of Starfell,* laying exactly where she'd last seen it—the book she hoped held the answers she was looking for.

"Fable?" Brennus whispered from above.

"Ssh!" She glared up at him, then pointed at him and mouthed, "Stay. Up. There." She jabbed the air with every syllable.

He peered down at her with wide eyes, a pale ghostly head in the frame of the vent hole, and nodded.

The scratching noises grew more frantic. It was a noise Fable recognized, something familiar. She wrinkled her nose and listened intently. What on earth could it be?

She got to her feet and walked slowly toward the desk. The noise grew louder as she got closer, but there was still no sign of what could be making it. She squinted at the nearby shelves, trying to make out the shapes. As far as she could tell, there was nothing out of place, she could hear no noises other than the frantic scritching from the desk.

Fable stood in front of the desk and bent towards the book to get a closer look. The cover twitched, ever so slightly, in rhythm with the scribbling noises. Carefully, Fable placed her hand on the cover.

The book sprang open, a soft light shining from its pages.

She jumped backwards and gave a small shriek, snapping her hand away in horror. Memories of smoky tentacles rushed back to her—but all she could see was the soft yellow glow from the pages.

This book was different. There was no smoke, no fire, no reaching tentacles. She edged closer and peered down at the luminous pages.

Words were being scrawled across them, written by an invisible hand. She recognized the sound now—a pen scratching the page. A familiar sound that Fable had heard thousands of times growing up when she watched her Aunt Moira sign school slips, fill out paperwork, and write Yuletide cards for the neighbours. A sound she had just heard back in Tulip Manor when Fedilmid had scribbled his letter to her aunt.

Fable Nuthatch nears the desk, her curiosity overcoming her fear. She jolts with surprise as she opens my cover, afraid of the worst. Now, gazing down into me, she's enchanted with wonder at the sight of a book writing itself. Only I know that she had better run. Scoot herself out of this room before Endora slams my cover shut in her face.

The writing stopped. Fable stared down into the book, the words taking a moment to register. Before she had a chance to recoil from the desk, the cover slammed shut, just as the words had said it would. Bony fingers with long, sharp blood-red nails held the cover closed. The lamp on the desk lit up, blazing into Fable's eyes. She tried to jump back, but the hand grabbed Fable's chin.

Endora forced Fable's face towards her. Blinking, Fable met her great-grandmother's gaze. A wide grin split Endora's crimson lips.

"Fable, it's so nice to see you."

The Shattering Glass

Fable jerked her head sideways, loosening Endora's grasp. She stumbled backwards. Endora laughed. The wicked sound rang through the library.

"I figured I would find you here. Stupid girl, did you think you could escape?"

Fable bumped into the shelf behind her. "What did you do to Timothy?"

"Timothy?" Endora tapped her fingers on her chin with a smirk. "The weak little boy my Collector took instead of you?" She crossed her arms. "I took his life, of course."

She flicked her wrist and Timothy's portrait appeared next to her, resting upright on the floor. She caressed the top of the frame.

"He wasn't completely useless, after all." She gazed into the mirror and ran a finger over her smooth cheek.

Fable stared at Timothy's picture and her stomach clenched. Laughing, Endora let go of the frame and the

213

heavy portrait fell face-first to the ground. Fable cried out in horror. The glass shattered in every direction.

"Timothy! No!"

Endora crunched a stilettoed heal into the broken fragments. "Have you made up your mind, child?" She loomed over Fable. "Are you going to stay with me, where you can be yourself and grow into your powers?"

"You said I'd have until tomorrow to decide." Fable shrank back further against the bookcase. The hard wooden shelf and the uneven edges of the book spines jabbed into her back. She had nowhere to go.

"I've changed my mind." Endora grabbed Fable's arms, pinning her to the shelf. She narrowed her amethyst eyes. There was no smile on her face now.

"You either choose to stay with me, or I'll lock you in that room and make you."

Endora's eyes burned, changing from purple to scarlet red. Sharp fingernails dug into her arms.

"You're hurting me!" Fable twisted away from the hag.

"This is nothing." Endora snarled. She shook Fable and slammed her into the shelf. "Try to escape, and you'll never see the light of day again."

Fable bit back a scream. She glanced at the grate in the ceiling. Brennus was nowhere to be seen. "What have you done with my friends?"

Endora's distorted, angry face melted into a false smile. "Your friends? Your friends are going to join their families. But I can see how much they mean to you, and I'm not completely heartless. Promise to stay, dear, and I'll let your friends go."

For a moment, Fable believed her. She desperately wanted to. She squeezed her eyes shut. Her head pounded, and her whole body ached. She couldn't bear the thought of her friends being trapped inside a picture, their life drained away like Timothy's.

"I—"

"No!" Brennus' voice echoed throughout the library. "It's a trick, Fable. Don't listen to her!"

Fable opened her eyes and peered around Endora. Brennus dropped to the ground from the ceiling above. Her heart leapt. *He's okay!*

Endora turned her head, still hunched over Fable and clutching her arms. She cackled, all pretence of graciousness disappearing in an instant. "Arame!"

Arame appeared inside the library beside Brennus, who jumped and backed away from the toad-man.

Arame gaped as he took in the scene before him, looking like he was getting ready to catch a fly. "Yes, mistress?"

"Call the guards." Endora squeezed Fable's arms

harder. "I think Fable needs to see what my powers are capable of—starting with her little friend here."

White-hot anger rose up from Fable's toes and expanded through her chest. She gritted her teeth.

Arame eye's bulged more than usual as he glanced back and forth between Brennus and Endora. He shifted his weight from one foot to the other.

"Arame!" Endora let go of Fable and whirled to face him, her face red. She pointed a blood-red nail at him. "I know where your children are. Remember that."

"M-mistress, please!" Arame folded his hands together, and he crouched down in submission. "Please. Don't makes me hurts anybody else."

While the two argued, a movement across the room caught Fable's eye. The knight in the portrait was on his feet. He motioned to Fable. She cocked her head as he patted the glass encasing his frame.

Magic. I need to break it with magic.

Endora hurled threats at Arame with narrowed eyes. "If you ever want to see those nasty tadpoles again—"

Fable shot her hand forward and a spark of purple electricity exploded from her fingertips. It hit the glass of the knight's portrait. A spiderweb of cracks splintered out from the point of impact, but it stayed in one piece.

So close.

Her breath caught as the knight reached back and grabbed his sword. In one quick movement, he heaved it over his head with both hands and smashed the sword into the glass. With an ear-splitting *crack*, it shattered into pieces over the desk.

Endora shrieked and tore her gaze away from Arame toward the fractured portrait. Her jaw dropped. "No! Do you know how hard I worked to capture him?" She spun back to Fable, eyes blazing.

At that moment, Brennus saw his opportunity and jumped. He tackled Arame to the floor.

"Argh!" Arame croaked.

The two hit the ground in a pile of flailing arms and legs.

"What is going on?" Distracted, Endora twisted to see the commotion.

Fable took her chance. Clenching her stomach, she snatched Endora's arm and screamed. A steady stream of white light burst from her body and slammed into Endora. With a look of shock on her face, Endora flew across the room and landed below the knight's broken portrait.

"Fable, stop!" her great-grandmother shrieked, a note of fear in her voice.

White light flowed through the air between them, blasting Endora like water from a fire hose. She rose, her hands raised in front of her like a shield, and took a struggling step forward.

I can do this. Be brave like Thorn. And my parents. Fable swallowed her fear and stared into Endora's twisted face.

"Fable, remember, I am your great-grandmother." Endora advanced another step. Red sparks shot from her hands as she tried to push the magic back. "I'm family."

"No. Timothy is family. Aunt Moira is family. Thorn and Brennus are family." Fable's eyes bored into hers. "You make people fear you. That's not love. You destroy families!" She pushed Endora further back towards the wall where the knight stood waiting in his frame, arms extended toward the lich.

"What are you going to do? Hold me here forever?" Endora's tone changed, taunting in false confidence. She leaned into her power and tried to push back, but her magic fizzled out in a red haze around her.

"No."

With a final push, Fable shot Endora back towards the knight. Endora screamed as he grabbed her around the waist. He heaved her up into the frame.

"No!" Endora shrieked, clawing at his arms.

Fable walked over to the portrait and looked at her, her hands still extended. Her great-grandmother struggled to break free from the knight's grip.

"Now!" she shouted at the knight, who spun and hurled Endora away from him, further into the canvas background. Flailing, she fell onto her back. The knight leapt from the frame, landing in a crouch in front of the desk.

"I'm free. Finally, I'm free!"

Before Endora could even regain her feet, Fable waved her hand over the broken glass on the desk, and the shards shot up into the air and pieced back together, melding into each other as though they had never been broken. In another breath, the glass slid neatly back into its frame.

Endora howled with rage from behind it. She scrambled to her feet and pounded both fists on the solid glass before her.

There was a hammering at the library door. Fable spun around. Somebody was trying to break in. The door broke off its hinges and crashed to the floor.

Arame yelped and stared at the doorway. The knight whirled, ready to spring.

Thorn stood in the entryway, gasping for breath. She looked at Fable with yellow eyes, then over at Brennus and Arame, who now sat peacefully side-by-side on the floor. The knight eyed her warily, but stayed put.

Brennus patted the toad-man's arm to reassure him and then waved at Thorn. "Thorn! We're okay."

The Folkvar strode into the room and picked Fable up in a massive hug. "I heard Endora, and screaming, and a loud bang."

"We're fine." Fable hugged her back and then slid to the ground. "Endora's trapped. We're safe now."

She glanced at the portrait. Endora sat with her back to them. Her shoulders were slumped, her head bowed.

Fable turned to the knight. He got to his feet, armour clanging, with a gleaming smile.

"Thank you, child. I've been trapped in there for so long, I'd given up hope of ever getting out. I am deeply indebted to you."

"You did all the work." Heat rose in Fable's cheeks. "Thank you for helping us. What's your name?"

"Sir Reinhard. Of Stonebarrow."

Thorn cleared her throat. "What about Timothy?"

Fable's heart jumped. Timothy! She hurried over to his portrait on the floor, glass crunching beneath her shoes. She lifted the stretched canvas and turned it over.

"His eyes move. He's still there. You can save

him," Sir Reinhard said.

Timothy looked up at her, still in the same crouching position.

"Timothy?" She sat down on her knees and looked him in the eye. "Are you okay?"

He blinked, and she felt a surge of joy course through her. She grinned, tears welling up in her eyes. Thorn, Brennus and Arame crowded around her. Sir Reinhard stood a few feet behind them, watching.

"I'm not sure how—" Fable began uncertainly, staring at Timothy's frozen image.

"Magic." Brennus jerked his chin at the painting. "You should know this by now."

Thorn nodded. "What he said."

Her friends' words sunk in and gave her strength. Fable reached down to grab Timothy's raised hand, which lifted from the canvas to meet hers. With no glass to separate them, she entwined her fingers with his. His hand was cold to the touch, stiff and lifeless, but his eyes blazed.

Light poured out from her into the painting. Timothy's hand grew warmer and softened. He gripped her fingers, and slowly, she pulled him towards her. Life returned to his body, one limb at a time, until he stepped out of the frame and into her arms.

"Timothy." Tears streamed down Fable's cheeks.

His arms tightened around her, and his pale face broke into a smile.

"Fable—" he began, then screamed.

A familiar red-clawed hand grasped his ankle, reaching from the canvas. Fable shrieked and tightened her grip around him.

"No!"

She kicked at the clawing fingers. Arame's rubbery hand grabbed hers. The world around her dissolved into darkness.

Home

A soft breeze swept across Fable's face. The sun beat down, warm on her body. Peace drifted over her. She opened her eyes and saw Timothy next to her in the grass, gazing up at the clouds. He looked over at her.

"Hey."

She gave him a small smile. "Hey, yourself."

He smiled back.

"Fable?" Aunt Moira's voice rang out through the air. "Timothy? Is that you?"

Her tranquility shattered, Fable sat up into a cloud of shimmery black tulle. She pushed the fabric out of the way. Her mind jolted and she turned her head, frantically calling for her friends. "Thorn? Brennus?"

"Right here." Thorn sat up, the braids and grass in her wild copper hair sticking out in every direction.

"Me, too." Brennus peered around Thorn.

"Children! Oh, my goodness."

The familiar voice tugged at Fable's heart.

223

"I think that lady's looking for you." Thorn pointed across the meadow.

Fable's gaze followed her friend's pointing finger. The pink flowers of Tulip Manor waved in the breeze. The blue door of the cottage hung open, and a woman in a long, flowing skirt was running in their direction.

Timothy and Fable both shouted at once.

"Mom!"

"Aunt Moira!"

Moira reached them and threw herself onto her knees. She scooped both children up into her arms. "I can't believe it's you! Both of you. You're okay." She kissed their heads and sobbed loudly. "I thought I lost you. I couldn't bear it."

Fable hugged her back. "We're okay. I missed you so much."

Timothy buried his head in his mother's embrace. He looked up at her. "How did you get here? Wait, how did *we* get here?"

"Arame," Brennus said.

A croak sounded nearby, and the smell of rotting cabbage met Fable's nose. Arame stood, hands clasped, in the tall grass in front of them.

Aunt Moira peered up at him. "Thank you, sir, for bringing my children back to me." She smoothed Timothy's hair back from his face and kissed him

224

again. "How can I ever repay you?"

Arame shifted, his eyes on the ground. "Ah, thanks Fable. Not me."

"No, really. Thank you, Arame." Fable held out a hand to him. He leaned forward and gently shook it.

She gazed past her friends, hoping to see sunlight glinting off the shine of metal armor. "Sir Reinhard— did he get out too?"

Arame shook his head, his bulbous eyes cast down. "No, he wasn't nears us when I grabbed you childrens. But I wouldn't worries too much. Now that he's out of the frame, I'm sures he can escapes the hag. He has his sword. He's very strong."

Fable swallowed the lump in her throat. She hoped he escaped, and that they would see him again.

"I must go." Arame looked around the meadow nervously. "My family. Endora knowses where theys are." He let go of her hand and, with a lick of his slimy pink tongue, he faded away before them, leaving a green haze where he had just stood.

"Endora?" Aunt Moira's face paled. "Did he say Endora?"

"She kidnapped all of us, but we broke free," Fable said.

Her aunt gasped, hugging Timothy tighter.

The colour drained from Timothy's face, and his

eyes welled up with tears. "I was trapped—but Fable and her friends saved me—" He broke off and let out a small cry.

Aunt Moira placed her cheek against his hair.

"She's on the loose again?"

"Yes, but—" Fable began, but Moira cut her off.

"We will discuss this more once we are safe inside." Aunt Moira stood, wiping the grass from her long skirt.

"Are Fedilmid and Algar home?" Fable asked, getting to her feet.

"Of course." Moira took Fable and Timothy's hands. She clutched them tightly, her face streaked with tears.

"You two, as well." She motioned to Thorn and Brennus. "Come along."

Fedilmid and Algar welcomed them all with hugs and cheers. Grimm was there, too. He bounded to the door and covered his children with sloppy, wet dog kisses.

"You're safe!" Fedilmid jumped up and down, his robe flapping around his legs.

"I can't believe you snuck out on us." Algar pursed his lips, but his eyes crinkled. He broke into an appreciative smile.

"I can." Fedilmid grinned, a mischievous twinkle in his eye.

Once they were safe inside Tulip Manor, Fedilmid and Aunt Moira went back outside and walked around the stone cottage. They waved their hands over the walls, singing a soft melody, and blue waves shimmered over the home. They'd explained that with Endora free, they felt it best to strengthen the regular safety enchantments on the home.

"We should now be invisible to any prying eyes wanting to do us harm." Fedilmid ushered Moira inside and placed the bar securely over the front door.

That night, after a thorough explanation of the events at Endora's mansion, they feasted. Algar served a five-star meal of roast venison, garlic mashed potatoes, Yorkshire pudding, a huge garden salad, and a variety of roasted vegetables for Thorn. He followed it up with heaping bowls of ice cream slathered with chocolate sauce.

Over dinner, Fable and her friends told the adults their story. The adults gasped and exchanged worried glances as they described Endora, her mansion, the portraits, the boars, and the raised dead she used as guards.

"And that book in the library . . ." Fable pushed away her empty ice cream bowl. "'*The Magic and Lore of Starfell.*' It writes itself. It was writing about me."

"It writes the history of Starfell as it happens,"

Fedilmid said. "It only writes the important bits. You must be very special." He winked.

"I wonder how she got a hold of it. It should be at the Ministry in Mistford," Algar said. "What is she planning?"

Aunt Moira pushed away from the table and gathered her dishes.

"It doesn't matter right now." She picked up Timothy's plate and ruffled his hair with her free hand. "My children are safe. And Fable . . ." She stopped beside her niece and took her hand. "I'm so sorry I tried to hide your magic. I thought it was for the best. I was afraid she would find us if word got out." She sniffled and released Fable's hand to wipe away a tear. "But she found you anyhow."

Fable blinked at her aunt, who stood and continued gathering bowls.

Her arms full of dishes, Aunt Moira walked to the kitchen and placed them in the sink. She turned on the tap, sniffled again and wiped her eyes.

Fable bit her lip and fidgeted with her hands under the table. *Sorry? She actually sees my side now?*

Brennus turned to Algar and Fedilmid and dove into the story of the galaxy under the stairs. "You wouldn't believe it! We sailed across on a door."

"He almost didn't make it onto the door." Thorn

elbowed him in the ribs. Timothy laughed and gazed at them both, his eyes bright and happy.

Fable slipped away from the table and joined her aunt at the sink. "I'm sorry for what I said. Back at Rose Cottage." She picked up a towel to dry the dishes that her aunt was scrubbing.

"It's okay, dear." Her aunt sighed. "I've been hard on you. I want you to know that I love you, just as much as Timothy. You're my child, too."

"I know." Fable dried a plate and stacked it neatly on the counter. "I love you, too."

Aunt Moira reached over and pulled Fable into a hug. They finished the dishes in silence, listening to Thorn and Brennus argue over the details of their capture.

"The boar closed in on me with its tusks flashing inches from my face." Brennus moved his hand across his throat in a slashing gesture.

Thorn rolled her eyes. "They weren't anywhere near you. If it weren't for me fighting off that guard in the driveway—"

"Fight him off? That whip just about killed you!"

Fedilmid and Algar laughed out loud, eyes twinkling and nodding their heads in encouragement.

"We haven't had a full house like this in ages." Algar grinned and he took a sip from his mug.

"Ages? We've lived here for forty years, and we've never had company like this," Fedilmid said. "Although . . ." He turned towards Moira and motioned her back over to the table. "It sounds like that's about to change."

"Oh, yes." Aunt Moira put down her cloth. She and Fable rejoined the group in the dining area. Fable sat down next to Thorn at the far end of the table.

Aunt Moira dried her hands on her apron. "Now that we know that Endora is aware of Rose Cottage, I've asked Fedilmid and Algar if we can stay here at Tulip Manor."

Fable's face lit up. "Yes!"

"You haven't even heard if we've agreed," Fedilmid said with a smile.

He looked at each face in turn, meeting Fable's gaze last. She held her breath, all the reasons he should probably say no filling her mind—not enough room, more mouths to feed, attracting angry hounds and an evil sorceress . . .

He winked at Fable. "Which we have. You're always welcome here."

Fable grinned and Timothy clapped his hands.

"It's temporary," Aunt Moira said. "For now, only until we sort this whole mess out."

Her words barely registered in Fable's mind. A new home. Outside of Larkmoor. Away from the bullies, the rules, and the fear. Tulip Manor.

Brennus shifted in his seat and looked down at his feet. Thorn's quivering lip gave away her forced smile.

Fable frowned. "What about Thorn and Brennus? They don't have homes to go to. We couldn't get Thorn's parents. And we didn't even find Brennus'." Her voice sounded like a croak in her ears.

"It's not your fault," Thorn stared at her hands on her lap, tears brimming her eyes. "I know my parents are gone. There was no life in that portrait."

Fable squeezed her friend's hand under the table.

After a moment of sad silence, Algar crossed his arms. "You know, I always need more help around here. Chopping wood, cleaning the chimney—"

"Oh, please, Algar." Fedilmid rolled his eyes and jumped to his feet. "They're welcome at Tulip Manor as long as they need a home. Now, more ice cream?"

Fable beamed as her friends chattered with excitement. She gazed around the table. Aunt Moira stood behind Timothy with her arms around his shoulders. Thorn and Brennus argued over the events at the Buttertub Tavern, while Algar listened with rapt attention. Fedilmid fussed in the kitchen, refilling their bowls. Grimm sat by his side, waiting for food to hit the floor.

Fable's heart was full. This was her home.

This was her family.

It was nearly midnight. The four children sprawled across the floor of the living area in Tulip Manor. Fable sat with her legs straight out in front of her, her mother's journal resting on her lap. She was wedged between Timothy and Thorn, who lay on her back with her arms behind her head. Like many other nights, her mind was on anything but sleep.

Timothy snored softly beside her, curled up under a down quilt, his lips curved in a smile. One hand rested on Fable's leg. She didn't push him off. She still couldn't believe he was next to her.

"I'm sorry about your parents," Fable said softly to her friend. "I wish we could have saved them."

"They were gone before we even got there." Thorn shook her head sadly. "There was nothing we could do."

"Your sister wasn't on the wall," Fable replied. "She's still out there. We can find her."

"I hope so." Thorn nodded. "Brennus' parents, too."

232

Their friend rustled quietly beneath his quilt on the other side of Timothy. He murmured something and rolled over in his sleep.

Thorn raised her head to look at Faari's journal. "That was your mom's?" she whispered.

"Yeah." Fable opened the notebook and flipped through some of the pages. "I can't believe I found it. It's full of stories about her and my dad. And Timothy's dad, too."

She gazed lovingly at the pages filled with drawings of odd, colourful flowers that her mother had seen in her travels with her father. Little notes on how they greeted her and the songs they sang were scribbled in the margins.

"Look at these. I'd love to find some. Faari Blossoms, like my mom." Fable ran her fingers over the vibrant purple blooms that filled the page. "Do you think there are any around Tulip Manor?"

"Maybe. Ask Algar tomorrow." Thorn turned towards the coffee table, which was jammed against the wall. On it rested Fable's book bag.

"Fable, your bag is shaking."

"What?"

Fable closed her mother's journal, set it aside and leaned forward to peer around her friend. Thorn was right. Her bag was vibrating. Or, rather, the book inside it was.

233

"No . . ." Fable pulled her knees to her chest, her hands shaking.

A soft light shone through the material. The bag vibrated to the edge of the small table and, before Fable could reach out to grab it, tumbled over the edge. As it fell and landed on the floor, the *Book of Chaos* slipped out and landed wide open.

Fable lunged at the book over Thorn's legs. She landed on her elbows with her face above the softly glowing pages. No smoke or scary tendrils curled from them. No heat blazed out at her.

As she stared at the page, a small line appeared. It slowly traveled across the blank space. It zigged and zagged across the page, growing into a drawing. Mountains, streams, and trees appeared before her eyes.

"What's it doing?" Thorn peered over Fable's shoulder.

"I think it's a map."

At the top right-hand corner of the page, between two jagged mountains, a crimson red star appeared. An invisible hand scrawled *The Blood Star* beneath it, along with the date *November 13*. Fable's birthday.

Fable and Thorn exchanged glances.

"This is a very un-book-like book," Thorn said.

Follow Fable's adventures in Starfell Book Two: The Guitar of Mayhem. Available now!

After their escape from Endora's mansion, Fable Nuthatch and her friends are recovering at Tulip Manor. With Fedilmid and Aunt Moira's protection spells keeping them safe, the children have settled into a routine life of friendship, studying, and practicing magic.

When odd messages appear in Fable's book and a strange light in the forest rouses her dog's curiosity, the children's lives are spun back into mayhem. A trip to the magical city of Mistford leads them on a wild chase after a rogue star, a missing astronomer, and an enchanted guitar that holds a secret that will change their lives forever.

With Endora hot on their trail, can Fable and her friends discover the truth before it's too late?

GLOSSARY

Algar Whimbrel (AL-gar WIM-bruhl) – a woodsman; Fedilmid's husband.

Arame (AIR-am) – a portal-caster; Endora's first assistant.

Brennus Tanager (bren-US) – Bart and Isla's son; Fable's best friend.

Burntwood Forest – forest on the east side of Starfell; previously the Greenwood Forest; where Fable landed when she first left Larkmoor.

Collector – a magical item enchanted to transport beings who set it off.

Endora Nuthatch (en-DOR-ah NUHT-hatch) – a lich; Morton's grandmother; Fable's great-grandmother.

Faari Nuthatch (FEH-ree NUHT-hatch) – Morton's wife; Fable's mother; deceased.

Fable Nuthatch (NUHT-hatch) – a sorcerer; Faari and Morton's daughter; Moira's niece; Timothy's cousin.

Fedilmid Coot (FEHD-ill-mid) – a witch; Algar's husband; also known as The Fey Witch.

firehawk – a wild chicken that breathes fire and reads auras; Star's species.

Folkvar (FOWK-var) – a giant race of people who live in colonies and off the land; Thorn's race.

Grimm – the Nuthatch's loyal mastiff.

Larkmoor – non-magical town separated from the rest of Starfell by the Windswept Mountains.

lich – a magic-caster who gains power by evil deeds; drawn to power to and immortality.

Lichwood – the forest on the west side of Starfell; where Tulip Manor resides.

Mistford – magical city in the south of Starfell.

Moira Nuthatch (MOY-ruh NUHT-hatch) – a witch; Thomas's wife; Timothy's mother; Fable's aunt.

Morton Nuthatch (NUHT-hatch) – Faari's husband; Fable's father; Endora's grandson; deceased.

Orchid (OR-kuhd) – a Folkvar; Thorn's sister.

Rose Cottage – Fable, Timothy and Moira's home in Larkmoor.

sorcerer – a person who's magic comes from within.

Star – a firehawk; Fable's first friend and guide in Starfell.

Stonebarrow – industrious city in the north of Starfell.

The Buttertub Tavern – a pub between the Burntwood Forest and the Lichwood; halfway between Mistford and Stonebarrow.

Timothy Nuthatch (NUHT-hatch) – Moira and Thomas's son; Fable's cousin.

Thomas Nuthatch (NUHT-hatch) – Timothy's father; Moira's husband; Morton's brother; deceased.

Thorn – a Folkvar; Fable's best friend; Orchid's sister.

Tulip Manor – Fedilmid and Algar's stone cottage in the Lichwood.

undead – corpses raised from their graves by a powerful magic-caster.

Windswept Mountains – mountain range that cuts across the west of Starfell.

witch – a person who draws magic from the earth.

wizard – a person who learns magic from books.

About the Author

An avid reader and writer since she was a child, Jessica Renwick inspires with tales of adventures about friendship, courage, and being true to yourself. She is the author of the award-winning *Starfell* series for middle-grade children.

She enjoys a good cup of tea, gardening, her pets, consuming an entire novel in one sitting, and outdoor adventures. She resides in Alberta, Canada on a cozy urban homestead with her partner, fluffy monster dogs, four chickens, and an enchanted garden.

You can find her at www.jessicarenwickauthor.com , on Instagram and Facebook @jessicarenwickauthor, and on Goodreads. Independent authors rely on word-of-mouth. A review on Amazon, Goodreads, or your choice of bookseller would be greatly appreciated. Just a few words really do make a big difference.

Made in the USA
Monee, IL
08 November 2022